KU-050-758

ACC. No: 02851010

Born in the UK, Heather has spent most of her adult life in Australia and now lives in Melbourne with her husband and daughter. A writer for more than twenty years, she is the author of *Flying Colours* and *Red for Danger*.

STARSHINE BLUE

Jimmy Flynn has devoted his life to the champion Starshine Blue, after rescuing him as a foal from a burning stable. Hiding the fact that he is really James Kirkwood Jr., son of a hotel magnate, he has no wish to be drawn into his father's business empire. Even after winning the heart of Leila Christensen, his boss's daughter, he keeps his true identity from her. But Leila does not like to be deceived and their fragile happiness is threatened when unexpected events force Jimmy's secret into the open and he must face up to the future his father planned.

Books by Heather Graves
Published by The House of Ulverscroft:

FLYING COLOURS
RED FOR DANGER

HEATHER GRAVES

STARSHINE BLUE

Complete and Unabridged

ULVERSCROFT
Leicester

First published in Great Britain in 2007 by
Robert Hale Limited
London

First Large Print Edition
published 2009
by arrangement with
Robert Hale Limited
London

British Library CIP Data

Graves, Heather
Starshine Blue.—Large print ed.—
Ulverscroft large print series: general fiction
1. Stablehands—Fiction 2. Stables—Australia—
Fiction 3. Hotelkeepers—Australia—Fiction
4. Family-owned business enterprises—Australia—Fiction
5. Secrecy—Fiction 6. Love stories 7. Large type books
I. Title
823.9′2 [F]

ISBN 978–1–84782–591–9

Published by
F. A. Thorpe (Publishing)
Anstey, Leicestershire

Set by Words & Graphics Ltd.
Anstey, Leicestershire
Printed and bound in Great Britain by
T. J. International Ltd., Padstow, Cornwall

This book is printed on acid-free paper

PROLOGUE

He was a beautiful foal, born to a stylish mare, once a champion in her own right. Now, having proved herself capable of reproducing her form and her talent, these days she was known as just Nula — an unremarkable, pale grey mare; a reliable dam who gave birth without difficulty and was always able to feed and raise her own foal.

The newcomer, having made his way into the world with the minimum of trauma, was welcomed and washed by his mother with long, warming strokes of her tongue. Having satisfied herself that he was whole and sound, the mare nudged him gently with her nose, encouraging him to stand on trembling, unsteady legs to take his first milk. As his coat dried, it became such a distinctive gunmetal shade of grey, it looked almost blue. And, instead of the white diamond common to so many horses, his forehead was marked with the shape of a shooting star, right across his nose. It gave his head an odd, lopsided appearance but was somehow endearing at the same time.

All this took place in the stables, under the

watchful gaze of Jim Kirkwood. Although this was by no means the first time he had seen a foal take its first breath, at seventeen he was still in awe of the miracle of birth. Seeing Nula's affection for her foal, it occurred to him yet again that he was as different from his father as it was possible for a young man to be. While he was devoted to these animals, understanding that they might have feelings and emotions not so different from his own, his father viewed them only in terms of dollars and cents. James Kirkwood Senior regarded his bloodstock ranch on the outskirts of the beautiful Tweed Valley as just one of his business enterprises, no more important to him than any of the rest. To his son, Jimmy, it was already so much more.

When his son returned from his final year of school with glowing reports, James had taken it for granted that he would go on to university and had already made enquiries at some of the better colleges. He wanted his son to be more than just a namesake, expecting him to be filled with the same dollar-hungry ambition and grow into a man of business like himself. He was at a loss to understand what he saw as his son's quaint obsession with the small world of Kirkwood's Lodge, no matter how prestigious or picturesque — the lush paddocks flanked by cane fields on one side and the marshy banks of the River Tweed on the other. Too restless to remain in one place for long and anxious to maintain a firm hold on his entire enterprise, James Kirkwood kept a light plane and a pilot in service to fly him anywhere in Australia at a moment's notice.

His son's rejection of a world he regarded as near perfect, came as a rude shock. He raised the subject of Jim's future as they relaxed on the verandah in the cool of an early summer's evening, sharing a bottle of ale before dinner, and he listened with mounting dismay as Jim told him how much he loved the Tweed Valley and had no intention of leaving.

'You don't have to worry about me, Dad.' He smiled at his father, having no inkling of the storm about to break over his head. 'I've always loved this place more than anywhere else in the world. I'll just stay on here and keep raising good horses for you.'

'No, Jim, I'm afraid that isn't an option. I can't let you turn your back on your future!' Too agitated to sit still, James stood up and paced the rustic verandah of the old homestead, waving a dismissive hand towards his own land. 'You can't mean to bury yourself here on this little farm. It's such a small part of our enterprise. We own hotels in most of the major cities, including the Gold Coast and I haven't scratched the surface yet. There's a whole world out there.'

'I know that, Dad, but I — '

'No buts. I need you to graduate in business studies and take up your rightful place — at my side.'

'Dad, I'm sorry to disappoint you but that's not what I want. It isn't the life for me. Sally's the one with the head for business — you know that. She graduated with honours. She's so much more like you than I am.'

'That's all very well but your sister's only a woman.' His father's views were old-fashioned and although he found Sally amazingly useful, he had no faith in the long-term value of women in business. 'She'll marry eventually and then she'll have children. She'll have no time for Kirkwood Enterprises then.'

'I wouldn't count on it,' Jimmy muttered. His sister was almost thirty now, without a boyfriend in sight and she had all the drive and ambition he lacked. He found it hard to picture Sally as the matriarch of a family.

'Jim, this is crazy.' His father returned to the original argument. 'Surely you're not going to waste those good grades? You can't bury yourself out here in the sticks as a stable hand?'

'But, Dad, this is what I love — working with horses. I'm not a city boy, I never have been. And I'm sorry if you didn't realize it till now. I just like it here. You can promote me to stable foreman if you like.'

'At seventeen? Hardly. Besides, we already have a perfectly good stable foreman who knows all there is to know about breeding horses,' James Kirkwood grumbled, staring at his son as if he had suddenly grown horns and a tail. He was a man used to getting his own way. Jim pressed home his advantage while his father seemed to be at a loss for words.

'And aside from anything else, I don't enjoy flying. I don't want to spend my whole life rattling up and down the country in that plane, like you do. I can't think of anything worse.'

'Well, thanks a lot. I've bred me a cissy here, have I?'

'I didn't say I was scared of flying, I just don't like it, that's all. I'm perfectly happy to stay on here. I'm sorry if it's not what you expected of me.'

'It certainly isn't. I expected a lot more from my only son. I can see now it was a mistake to let you spend so much of your free time with the horses.' He shrugged, dealing with the problem and dismissing it. 'Stay here and rot, then, if that's all you want. I'm sure Sally will be more than happy to step into the breach.' He said this, hoping to ignite a spark of ambition in his son. But Jim only smiled, knowing this to be true. All it needed was for their father to start appreciating his sister's talents.

'I wish you had half her drive,' his father growled. 'I need a good man at my side to help me build a solid future to leave to the two of you.'

'Hold it right there, Dad. I know what you're up to. You're trying to make me feel guilty enough to give in. Well, this time it's not going to work.'

More harsh words passed between them and they parted on bad terms, Jim going to eat his meal in the kitchen rather than joining his father at the dinner table. If they were to spend any more time together now, he knew they would only quarrel again. James was due to fly out to Melbourne first thing in the morning. Perhaps, when he had time to reflect and had got over his disappointment, he might begin to see his son's point of view.

Jim was a heavy sleeper and the smell of smoke and burning hay was slow to penetrate the nightmare that held him in its grasp. He was dreaming of the Middle Ages, of the blood-red robes of the Inquisition and people screaming and struggling as they burned at the stake, their tormentors piling on more logs to build up the fire. He moaned restlessly in his sleep, covering his head with his pillow to shut out these disturbing sounds. Suddenly, he awoke with a start, realizing it wasn't human screams he was hearing at all but the high-pitched whinnying of terrified horses and the thud of their hooves as they tried to kick their way out of their stalls.

He leaped out of bed, cursing and throwing on the same clothes he had taken off only hours before. A glance out of the window told him the hay loft at one end of the stable block was on fire — all the more dangerous at this time of year when the weather had been so hot. He ran the length of the sprawling homestead screaming 'Fire! Fire!' to alert the rest of the household.

While the stable foreman and his son went into their drill to contain the blaze, he wrapped a wet cloth around his face and rushed into the stables to release as many horses as he could, his first concern for Nula and her newborn foal. Fortunately, her stall wasn't close to the fire, although smoke billowed through the stables, disorienting him and making it hard to breathe, let alone see.

He lifted the foal in his arms and staggered outside, knowing Nula would follow, and secured them both in a paddock nearby. Then he went back to see what more he could do. He rescued several more mares and a stallion, affected by smoke, and was dismayed to see that others had injured their legs in their panic to free themselves from their boxes.

With the stable foreman and the boys all fighting it, the fire was quickly contained although a plume of smoke still drifted skywards from the ashes. The foreman's son offered to stay and keep watch and stamp out any stray sparks that might reignite the blaze.

In the morning, his father was up early, surveying the damage with a critical eye. Jim found him conferring with the vet who carried a rifle under his arm, looking grim. He hurried over to join them.

'What's that for?' He glanced at the gun, his suspicions immediately aroused.

'Now, Jimmy, don't make a fuss.' His father made a placating gesture with his hands, taking him to one side. 'Doc Parsons is here to deal with the wounded horses. Just let him get on with his job.'

'But you don't have to put them down, surely? They can mend.'

'No room for sentiment in business, Jim. You're old enough to know that. These animals aren't pets. What use is a racehorse with damaged limbs? And most of the mares we have now are already too long in the tooth. Well past their prime.'

'I nearly got scorched myself, getting them out of there. Are you trying to tell me I did it for nothing?'

' 'Fraid so.' His father shrugged. 'You were brave but fool-hardy. But you'll see, it'll work out OK.' He rested a hand on his son's shoulder and lowered his voice. 'The insurance will more than cover our losses. We can make a fresh start with new stock.'

Jim wrenched himself free to stare into his father's face. 'You sound almost pleased this has happened. I'm beginning to wonder if you arranged it.'

'Shut up, you insolent pup!' James grabbed his son's elbow and squeezed it hard enough to make him wince as he drew him to one side to speak through gritted teeth. 'Let that sort of talk get around and the insurance people won't pay.'

'Good. I hope they don't,' Jim yelled, once more disengaging himself from his father's grasp and closing his eyes against the pain of hearing the sharp crack of the vet's mercy-killing gun. He didn't want to see the carcasses of his old friends thrown into the back of a truck to be taken to some pet's meat factory. Tears threatened and his first idea was to run back to the house, until he was struck by a fearful thought. He changed direction, running across to the paddock where Nula was standing protectively over her foal, ears back as she sniffed the air, disturbed by the gunshots.

'Don't you worry, girl.' Jim patted her neck, soothing her. 'I won't let anything happen to you — or your foal. That shooting star is going to be lucky for both of us, you'll see. Starshine Blue — that's what we'll call him. He's going to be my responsibility from now on, wherever my worthless father decides to sell him. I shall stay with him for the rest of his working life.'

1

2006

It was a cold morning, a strong breeze blowing off the sea and rattling the windows, making Leila shiver and snuggle back into bed, pulling the covers over her head when the alarm went off. It was still so dark it was hard to believe it was morning; no wonder she was reluctant to get out of bed. Still only half awake, she lay there thinking about her on-off relationship with Brett Hanson, thinking she really must stop being such a coward and find the courage to break it off for good.

Although she and Brett had both grown up on the island knowing each other by sight, they didn't get together until they met at a party when they were both sixteen. It had been love at first sight — or so she had thought at the time. Now she wondered if they were merely healthy young people in lust? A little older now and disillusioned with Brett's behaviour she was no longer sure.

Of course, Brett couldn't help that he was the walking, talking embodiment of every teenage girl's dream. He operated a tourist fishing boat for his father; work that went a long way towards keeping his tanned, muscular body in shape. Not many men could boast a six pack like Brett's, a pair of cornflower-blue eyes that twinkled with sexual promise and a shock of sun-streaked, surfie-blond hair. No wonder so many girls discovered a sudden interest in catching fish.

And when he strayed, which was often, they quarrelled and she would break it off. In a small local community like theirs, it was inevitable that she would find him out.

'Come on, Leila,' he would say, looking pained. 'You know it's you that I love. These girls mean nothing to me.'

'Then why take up with them? Why do you need them?' she'd say, choking back tears. 'It makes me feel so small and I hate it when people feel sorry for me.'

'Those girls don't have anything to do with my feelings for you.' He'd shrug. 'They're just a bit of icing on the cake — something to relieve the boredom of the daily grind on Dad's boat. But if it upsets you, I won't do it any more.' And at the time he would mean it — until someone new came along and it happened all over again.

Everyone, including Brett, assumed they would marry eventually but lately, she wasn't so sure. If he could cheat on her now, how could she trust her future to him or believe he would ever stop? But still the relationship limped on. She hadn't yet found the courage to do the right thing.

Her father's voice intruded on the sleepy reverie, breaking the daydream. 'Come on, Leila, let's be having you — it's nearly six o'clock.'

'Sorry, Pa,' she managed to croak, wishing she had the energy to leap out of bed with the same enthusiasm as he did. She wasn't an early morning person at all.

A country horseman of the old school, her father didn't believe in such luxuries as air conditioning and central heating. In his opinion they were decadent if not downright unhealthy and he didn't think a body needed to be too warm or too comfortable when it was lying in bed. From time to time when she raised the subject of modernizing and heating the homestead in winter, he would insist that the old Aga in the kitchen was quite enough. He would go on then to tell stories of harsh, European winters and she would tease him gently about his spartan Scandinavian upbringing.

'Welcome to the twenty-first century, Pa. Just because you used to roll naked in the snow and flog yourself with a bunch of damp twigs, doesn't mean the rest of us need to suffer now.'

'That never happened where I grew up,' Knud Christensen grinned. 'It's one of the great Scandinavian myths. Although we did have to break the ice on the lake in winter before we could swim.'

'You did not! You would have drowned — ' she began until she saw the dimples appearing on either side of his mouth, his blue eyes twinkling with good humour as he teased her in return.

She showered briefly to wake herself, dressed and went downstairs to join him in the kitchen where she could smell freshly brewed coffee.

'Your porridge is already out on the kitchen table,' he said. 'It's getting cold.'

'Thanks, Pa.' She smiled at him. She adored Knud who had been both father and mother to her since she was four years old when her mother, Inga, took off for South America with a visiting Argentine horse trainer. Leila, now twenty-one, could remember little about her mother except she had always smelled good, had a gentle voice and large grey-green eyes just like her own. Inga's looks were exceptional — everyone said so; she was a typical Scandinavian beauty with a porcelain complexion and luxuriant, silver-blonde hair. Certainly unusual enough to tempt the wealthy man from Argentina who lost no time in stealing her away from the easygoing Knud.

There were times when Leila saw occasional glimpses of that same beauty in the mirror, although she knew she would never measure up in style and poise to the woman who wrote irregularly and sent extravagant gifts to the daughter she had deserted. Sometimes, she would send photographs of herself, her new husband and their life in South America. These images meant nothing to Leila — it was like looking at a stranger; she could find nothing familiar in the snapshots of this well-groomed, middle-aged city-dweller, her silver hair scooped up into a cottage-loaf bun.

The truth was that Leila took more after her father. A country girl, born and bred, she had inherited little of her mother's stunning good looks, apart from those large, grey-green eyes. And, instead of her mother's remarkable silver-blonde mane, she had ordinary ash-blonde hair just like the gentle giant who was her father.

'What's up? Why are we in such a hurry today?' she said as she took her place at the table, spooning cream and honey on to her porridge as Knud passed her a cup of coffee. 'No one's booked for the races and the boys can take care of the track work, can't they?'

'Have you forgotten?' Giving his attention to his own porridge, Knud was avoiding her gaze. 'That new horse is arriving today.'

Leila's spoon clattered to her plate and she fixed her father with a stern look. 'What new horse, Pa? What have you done? We've already talked about this. I thought we agreed that although he's a champion, there were too many minuses and we weren't going to take him after all?'

'I changed my mind.'

'You mean Clive Bannerman changed it for you. Too soft you are by half. At this rate we'll end up with a stable full of old crocks.'

'Now that's enough. Starshine Blue is a champion and a long way from being an old crock — '

'Maybe.' She shrugged. 'But he's still eight years old. D'you really think Bannerman would part with him if he thought there was any money left to be made?'

'Clive and I go back a long way.'

'Giving him the perfect excuse to put one over on you.'

'It's not like that. Bannerman told me himself that in a big operation like his, he hasn't the time or the patience to train up a stayer. He prefers young, fresh horses who'll bring him a quick return.'

'Yeah. Dumping the old crocks on his good old mate, Knud.' She frowned as something occurred to her. 'How much did you pay for him, Pa?'

'Probably not enough. Eight is nothing — not these days. A ten-year-old won the Rubiton Stakes this year.'

'That was an exceptional horse.'

'Yes. Just like this one.'

'Lets hope so,' she said, chewing her lip. 'And there's something else I remember about Starshine Blue. He comes with strings attached, doesn't he? Has his own personal strapper?'

'So I believe.'

'Pa, we can't do this. We're a small operation and have enough strappers already. We can't afford to take on any more. And no one deserves to be sacked to make room for him.'

'Nobody's going to be sacked. Old Bobby Johnson has a bad back. He told me he's been thinking of retirement for some time — it's just a question of when. He wants to go and run a bait shop with his cousin in Ballina. Jimmy Flynn comes with the horse and, you'll see, it'll work out well for everyone all round.'

'Jimmy Flynn,' Leila repeated thoughtfully. 'Is that an Irish name?'

'I dunno. But lots of horsemen come from Irish stock.' At last Knud was becoming impatient with her questions. 'He's young but he's a good man, Clive says.'

'Clive would.' Leila was still unimpressed.

'No, he said he was sorry to lose him but Flynn insists on staying with the horse.'

She considered this, still suspicious as something occurred to her. 'You haven't even met the man, have you? How d'you know he'll fit in? What position is he going to hold here?'

'He'll take over as stable foreman when Bobby's shown him the ropes.'

'You want to bring in someone new — someone you haven't even met — and put him in over the lads? What about Bill Johnson? He expects to take over as foreman when his father retires.'

'Bill Johnson's heart isn't in it. He's a piss pot — too fond of his beer,' he said, making Leila raise her eyebrows. For Knud this was an uncharacteristic lack of charity.

'All the same, the boys aren't going to like it, Pa.'

'Then they can lump it, can't they?' A sound outside made him go to the kitchen window and look out. 'Damn. Looks like he's here already. An' I wanted to make sure the stables were shipshape before he came.'

'Whatever for? That's like polishing the house from top to bottom before a new cleaning lady arrives. He's the one who needs to impress us — not the other way about.'

'Now, Leila, please don't start . . . ' Knud put a steadying hand on her shoulder. He knew how stubborn she could be and didn't want her to take a set against the young man. They both watched as he drove both his four wheel drive and the horsebox into one of the spaces in the small car park outside.

'Look at that. He drives a Toyota four wheel drive — a Prado Grande, no less.' Leila rolled the Spanish-sounding words off her tongue. 'Take it from me, Pa, that's no ordinary strapper. How can he afford such a car? And do look, he's actually wearing a stetson.' She smothered a giggle as a tall, slim figure climbed out of the car and set the hat on his head at a jaunty angle before striding towards the back door. With a last warning glance at his daughter, Knud flung it open before the man had time to knock.

'Jimmy Flynn,' he said, vigorously shaking the newcomer's hand. 'Welcome to Ocean's View.'

'Mr Christensen? Nice to meet you at last.'

'Call me Knud — we don't stand on ceremony here. And this is my daughter, Leila.'

Leila, still feeling piqued that her father should have bought Starshine Blue and employed Flynn against her better advice and judgement, was surprised to look up into the warmest brown eyes she had ever seen. A lanky six-footer, Flynn was probably no more than a few years older than herself but his face was already scored with small laughter lines around the eyes; the sunburned face of a man who spent most of his time out of doors, squinting into the sun. He took off his hat with a flourish and subjected her to the full force of his smile. From his lazy, cowboy stance, she could tell he was a good rider although much too tall ever to have thought of becoming a jockey. He was not in the least as she had expected. But then what had she imagined him to be? What sort of man would devote his whole life to one horse? Some sort of crank, she had thought. A wizened gnome who would probably want to sleep near the animal in the stables. But Flynn was obviously nothing of the sort. His country clothes were of the best quality and he was obviously comfortable with who he was and the life he had chosen. The last thing Leila had expected was to feel an instant connection with the man, a jolt of attraction as his gaze quickly measured her up in return, bringing colour to her face and causing her heart to step up its beat.

How stupid is that? she mentally scolded herself. *How green are you, Leila? Allowing yourself to be bowled over by the smile of a handsome man. He knows exactly what effect that smile has on a girl and you're way too sensible to be taken in like that.*

'Sit down. Make yourself at home.' Knud gestured towards the kitchen table. 'Leila, pour some coffee for the lad. Have you eaten?'

'Not yet. Some toast and jam would be most welcome — soon as I've settled Bluey into his new quarters and given him a drink. He doesn't mind travel but he doesn't like being cooped up once we've arrived.'

'Of course,' Knud said as they both followed Jimmy outside.

He unfastened the horsebox and with several encouraging words to the horse, brought him out into the yard, still wearing his leg wraps from the journey. At the same time, Bobby Johnson and some of his lads came out of the stable to take a look. Bluey, ever ready to play to an audience, raised his head and sniffed the sea air as he looked around, taking in his new surroundings.

'But he's beautiful,' Leila whispered, forgetting her earlier misgivings as she moved forward to get acquainted with the horse, tracing the shape of the shooting star with her finger. 'And what an amazing colour — he really is almost blue. Where are we going to put him, Bobby?' She thought it only polite to ask the stable foreman.

'Well,' Bobby said slowly. 'He's a big fella so he's goin' to need a bit o' space. I s'pose we'd better give him the double box at the end as he's goin' to be the star of the show. I'm Johnson, by the way,' he said, introducing himself to Jimmy. 'We'll get the horse settled and then you can meet the rest of the lads.'

The lads had been more taken with Jimmy's blue Toyota than with the horse. They folded their arms and exchanged meaningful glances, suspicious of this new arrival who seemed to have so much more in the way of material possessions than they had. Even the horsebox looked brand new. Ignoring their less than friendly stares, Jimmy grinned at them briefly and followed Bobby into the stable with the horse.

Having assured Johnson that he preferred to see to the needs of his horse on his own, Jimmy had time to mull over his own first impressions. He knew at once that he would get on well with Knud Christensen, he already sensed that they were on the same wavelength. He wasn't so sure about the daughter who seemed a bit of an ice queen, appraising him through those beautiful, all-seeing eyes. For all that, she was impressive — her height and the strength of her jawline making her handsome rather than pretty. A Nordic princess with the figure of an Amazon and grey-green eyes like tropical waters just before a storm. He should take care. A man might drown in such eyes. He pulled himself up short. He had no business to be assessing Miss Christensen in that way. He had run foul of trainers' daughters before — Clive Bannerman's daughter, Dianne, to be precise.

He thought back to the time he left home to join Bannerman's stables. How naïve and gullible he had been. Bluey was just two years old and well grown, ready to leave the comfort of the Tweed Valley and his easygoing lifestyle to go into training. So, when Nula conveniently died of a heart attack around the same time, Jimmy's father nurtured the hope that his son would come to his senses and detach himself from the promise he made to remain with Starshine Blue. And when a prestigious trainer like Clive Bannerman was sufficiently impressed to pay a high price for the stallion, almost the last of Nula's line, Kirkwood believed the connection between his son and the horse would be broken. He couldn't have been more wrong.

‘If you’re selling Bluey to Bannerman, I’ll have to go with him.’ Calm but determined, Jimmy faced up to his father.

‘Don’t be ridiculous!’ Kirkwood’s temper exploded instantly. ‘Bannerman won’t want you — he has plenty of boys already.’

‘Then you’ll have to tell him I go with Starshine Blue or the deal’s off. Bluey’s special — any fool can see that. If Bannerman wants the horse badly enough, he’ll take me with him.’

‘You’ll make me a laughing stock. My son, the stable hand.’

‘All right. Who needs to know that I’m Kirkwood junior? I’m certainly not going to tell them. I’ll use Mum’s maiden name — Flynn — if that makes you feel any better. Who’s going to make a connection between you and a strapper called Jimmy Flynn?’

His father looked away, hiding the tears that always sprang to his eyes when anyone mentioned his wife. Moira had been the love of his life and when she drowned in a freak accident, caught in a rip while swimming on the Gold Coast, he had never allowed another woman to get close enough to take her place. Jimmy had been away at boarding school at the time and his father didn’t even make the effort to tell him; the reality was that he couldn’t, he would have broken down.

Instead, the boy had returned home to find his mother mysteriously absent and his father changed into this volatile stranger. It was left to his older sister, Sally, to tell him the truth, driving yet another rift between himself and his father. It seemed they were destined to misunderstand each other.

'You won't be able to keep it a secret,' Kirkwood said at last, shaking his head. 'It's too good a story — sure to get out.'

'I don't think so,' Jimmy assured him. 'It won't be the first time I've slipped under the radar. I've always been a bit of a hermit, even at school — no really close friends. And Bannerman's stables are hundreds of miles away, south of Sydney. Starshine Blue will be getting all the attention; not his strapper.'

'But what about the boys here?' Kirkwood nodded towards his lads who were pretending to work while covertly watching the earnest conversation between father and son. 'They'll know.'

'Not if we tell them I'm going to university, after all.'

So, he had left home, gone to Bannerman's stables and taken up an entirely new life. Even his appearance was changed. As Kirkwood Junior he'd had a clean-shaven, college-boy look with a side parting in his short, dark hair. Now he had given up the parting and allowed his hair to grow longer until it fell in a shaggy uneven mess almost to his shoulders. For a while he'd even sported an overgrown moustache until somebody told him it made him look like a Mexican bandit.

Clive Bannerman knew a competent horseman when he saw one and made good use of Jimmy Flynn who was given other horses to look after as well as Starshine Blue. Unfortunately for Jimmy, although he wasn't exceptionally good looking, having his father's hawkish nose, he had an attractive, loose-limbed walk and a charismatic smile, so it wasn't long before he came to the attention of Clive's daughter, Dianne.

He closed his eyes against the clear memory of Dianne, lying naked in his bed, her abundant dark hair spread like seaweed across his pillow, her dark brown nipples engorged and peaked with desire as she smiled and held out her arms to draw him in. She had been his first experience and for a while he had thought he was in love. After his sheltered upbringing, he found Dianne's amorous overtures irresistible and, at nineteen, was more than ready to be seduced. Naïvely, he had believed that he himself was the seducer until the stable foreman, Tom Kelso, took him aside and set him straight.

'I'd be careful of that one, Jimmy. If she

says she's in love with you, don't believe it. She's had every good-looking lad in the stables and some of the ugly ones, too.'

Although he was shocked to hear it, when Jimmy thought dispassionately of Dianne's behaviour, he knew it was true. She had a predator's gaze and was always preening, smiling and looking over his shoulder for someone new.

'So, what should I do?'

'Cool it, lad. And sooner rather than later. If Bannerman finds out you're on with his daughter, he'll have you out of here so fast, your feet won't touch the ground. And you're too good to lose. The girl may be a slut but her father has greater ambitions for her than to marry a stable hand.'

In passing, Jimmy wondered what Bannerman would have said if he'd known Jimmy Flynn was one of the heirs to the Kirkwood millions. But he heeded the foreman's advice and let the relationship with Dianne die a natural death. It wasn't long before he realized he'd had a lucky escape. And now, six years on, older and wiser, he was here at Knud Christensen's pleasant but very much smaller operation. And there was one thing he could see from the outset — Leila Christensen was cut from a very different cloth.

His mobile started to ring, intruding on his

thoughts and he smiled, answering a call from his sister, Sally.

'Sal, good to hear from you. How're things in the world of business?'

'More importantly, how are *you*? Are you there already? What's it like?'

'Hold on, I haven't even seen where I'm sleeping yet. We've only just arrived.'

'Bluey all right on the journey?'

'He's a trooper, you know that. I think he was a bit disappointed we didn't end up at a racecourse.'

'How d'you find the Christensens? Will you like working with them?'

'Yes, I think so,' he said slowly. 'It'll be very different from Bannerman's. Bit early to say.'

'You don't sound too sure.'

'Sally, stop being a mother hen. I've only just got here and I can't really talk just now.' He caught sight of Bobby Johnson waiting to speak to him. 'I'll call you back tonight when I've got more time.'

'You'd better,' his sister said crisply, ringing off.

Bobby Johnson was friendly, and happy to show Jimmy around the quarters that would be his when he took over as stable foreman. Like many of the early homesteads in Victoria, Ocean's View was really two houses; the first a plain but serviceable cottage, built for the purpose of housing the family while the larger, more impressive homestead was under construction. Nearly all of the casual help lived out but Johnson, his wife and son, Billy, occupied the cottage and, for the time being, Mrs Johnson was prepared to rent Jimmy the small spare room.

'We can leave you most of the furniture in the house, if you want to buy it?' She was quick to take advantage of the situation when Jimmy confessed he had no furniture of his own. 'We don't want much for it, do we, Bobby? And it's not worth the expense of shifting to Ballina.'

'I'll be happy to take it,' Jimmy said. He didn't like their ponderous, old-fashioned furniture but he thought he could change it gradually when they were gone. 'Long as Bluey and I settle in OK and Mr Christensen's happy with us.'

'He will be.' Bobby grinned. 'Knud's pretty easygoing and one of the strong, silent types but he'll have seen you know your way around horses. Unlike my son,' he said not without bitterness. 'He's happy only when he's bending his elbow at the pub.'

Jimmy smiled, thinking it tactful to ignore Bobby's last remark. 'I am good with horses, yes, but you can't go by Bluey. He and I have a special relationship — I was there with his mother when he was born.'

'You don't say? You've been there with him right from the start. You must know it's unusual for a lad to stay with one horse all this time?'

Jimmy nodded, reminding himself to be more discreet. He had never said much at Bannerman's about his earlier life, allowing them to assume he was of itinerant gypsy stock. He would let them fabricate just such a story here. Johnson cut across his thoughts, speaking again.

'I wish my son was more interested in horses than beer. He'll have to buck his ideas up when we're gone.'

'Then he's not going with you?' Jimmy's heart sank a little at the thought of continuing to work with the present foreman's sullen, overweight son.

'No fear.' Bobby smiled grimly. 'My cousin made it very clear. Myrtle and I will be welcome but he won't have Billy anywhere within cooee of him.'

Jimmy smiled at the old-fashioned expression.

* * *

Later, Knud came and leaned over the stable door, appraising Bluey after Jimmy had brought him back from a walk on the beach and a short swim in the sea. But although the sun had been shining brightly enough to tempt him, he discovered the wind still had a high chill factor. Even there on that empty beach, they had been chased by a racing reporter and his photographer, anxious to make a story out of Starshine Blue settling into his new home. Jimmy had pulled his baseball cap well down over his eyes and tried to stand behind the horse.

'No, come on — we want to see you, too,' the reporter urged. 'The old champion's loyal strapper — Jimmy Flynn, isn't it?'

'Yeah,' he had said, giving them as little as possible and not caring if they thought him an oaf.

'And how is the horse's stamina?' Christensen broke in on his reverie as he watched Jimmy's affectionate grooming of the horse.

'Fair,' Jimmy said honestly. 'At the moment he's under-raced. Clive hasn't been doing much with him for some time. But I've kept him fit enough and if we start him on a regular programme of track work, he'll spring right back into form. He isn't a lazy horse. He loves to train and he's always competitive in a race.'

'Do you ride him yourself?'

'I used to. Not so much now. I prefer him to get used to a lighter weight.'

'Leila rides track work for us. She's tall but she's light. Will she do?'

'Why not? Bluey has no vices. Even though he hasn't been gelded.'

'Yes, I was wondering about that.' Knud rubbed his chin. 'Always a good thing if you can keep a champion entire. Too many of them end up being gelded to focus their minds on racing rather than mares.'

'It's no secret that Clive wanted it done. He's a very immediate person and it's always hard to make him take the longer view. It nearly happened, too. The first and only time I left Bluey alone. Had to go to Sydney to visit family — it was my father's fiftieth birthday and he wanted me there.'

'Oh? What does your father do? Is he a horseman, like you?'

'He's in business,' Jimmy said dismissively, reminding himself once again to keep his private life private.

'Sorry. I didn't mean to pry. We were talking of Starshine Blue.'

'Yes. Dianne Bannerman promised to look after him for me. I never got to the bottom of what really happened as no one would tell it straight but I gather Dianne was fooling around in his stable with one of the lads.'

Knud rolled his eyes. 'You don't have to say any more.'

'You know about her, then?'

'Let's say I've experienced her mode of attack. She had a flattering opinion of Scandinavian men an' I had to set her straight. But go on — she was fooling around in Bluey's stall with one of the lads?'

'Well, nobody's quite sure how it happened but somehow they must have stumbled into the horse. He kicked out and broke Dianne's leg. Clive's knee-jerk reaction was to send for the vet and have him gelded to curb his bad temper. Luckily, I arrived home before the deed could be done. I had to talk fast and furious to stop Clive because he was all for it. Fortunately, the stable foreman backed me up and said Dianne's injury was nobody's fault but her own. That set Clive back a bit but he saved face by reminding me that he'd paid good money for the horse and if he saw fit to have him gelded later on, he'd bloody well do so. He topped it off by saying that if I didn't like his methods, I could leave.' Jimmy shook his head. 'I never left Bluey again. I was always half scared that I'd come back and find him gelded.'

Knud smiled and patted Jimmy on the shoulder. 'Well, you needn't live in fear of that happening here.'

2

The following day, Jimmy was awake early. He had spent a restless night as the Johnsons' spare bed had little to recommend it, having rusted springs that creaked whenever he moved and a mattress with a hollow in the middle, making him wonder how many bodies must have slept on it before. He promised himself that as soon as the Johnsons left, he would order himself a new bed.

He got up and stretched, hoping a hot shower would put his aching muscles to rights and planning on paying a visit to Bluey before catching up with the Christensens. Instead, he found Knud at the stables before him, laughing as the stallion looked out and bellowed a greeting to Jimmy.

'It's all right, Bluey, I haven't deserted you.' He patted his old friend on the neck and reached for a shovel to clear the pile of manure he had dropped during the night.

'No need for you to do that — mucking out is Bill's job,' Knud started to say but Jimmy had caught everything neatly on the shovel and was already taking it outside to add to the load in a skip provided by a local garden centre. He felt a momentary pang of sympathy for Bill Johnson. No wonder he had so little enthusiasm for the job if his main duty lay in keeping the stables clean.

'Come and have breakfast up at the house,' Knud invited when he returned. 'If I know Myrtle, she won't have offered you more than a cup of instant coffee and a piece of toast, if that.'

'I really ought to be catering for myself,' Jimmy muttered, thinking of the greasy, unappetizing lamb stew the Johnsons had offered for dinner the night before and how he'd excused himself, professing to be largely a vegetarian and taking only the vegetables that accompanied it.

'You've quite enough to do here without catering for yourself. Until you get settled into your own routine, you're eating with us.'

'Oh? But won't Leila . . . ?'

'Don't you worry about her. I do at least as much cooking as she does. After breakfast, I'll get her to show you around. We've only five horses in work at present and that includes Starshine Blue. Bobby and I are taking a couple of them to Cranbourne Races today. Not that we have particularly high hopes. They're just two-year-olds and pretty untried, but the owners are getting impatient to see them raced. In any case, they'll need to get used to the noise and general atmosphere of the track.

When they returned to the house, Leila was already at work in the kitchen. A smell of freshly brewed coffee greeted them and she had a pan of freshly picked mushrooms sizzling on the stove ready to be added to the omelette mixture she was whisking nearby. Jimmy's stomach growled in response, making her smile.

'Won't be long,' she said. 'You'll find the mugs in there.' She nodded towards the cupboard behind him. 'And there's milk in the fridge. Pour the coffee and I'll have the omelettes ready in a moment.'

Her omelettes tasted as good as they looked — light, fluffy and served with chunks of homemade bread full of sunflower seeds. Jimmy spread his with butter and tried not to wolf it but he was starving after his meagre supper of the night before.

After breakfast, Knud left, asking Leila to finish showing Jimmy around. Although the sun was shining brightly, there was no warmth in it at this hour of the morning and the wind was chill. He was glad of the warm clothing he had brought with him from Bannerman's. Further inland, the morning temperatures had often been below freezing. He'd expected the climate of Phillip Island to be a lot milder but hadn't allowed for the cool breeze blowing off the sea — sometimes it felt as if it were coming straight from the South Pole.

'This is Party Animal.' Leila showed him a handsome bay gelding. 'We're especially proud of him. He's already done well in the country and we have him booked to race in the city next month.' She moved on to the next stall. 'And this is Dreamy Princess — she's owned by a syndicate of six girls who keep her for the fun and the interest rather than the prize money she's going to make. Even so, she's capable of surprising us with the odd win.' The mare snickered and sniffed Leila's pockets, searching for a treat until Leila produced a peppermint.

'Surely that's bad for her?' Jimmy frowned.

'Of course.' Leila grinned, her face alive with mischief as the mare lifted it daintily from her hand. 'But don't you like to have something that's bad for you once in a while?'

Yet again Jimmy felt the jolt of attraction which had taken him by surprise the day before. He changed the subject, moving to safer ground. 'You're quite a distance from any of the local tracks. Why did your father choose to have his stables down here?'

'Quality of life, Pa says; he's lived near the sea all his life. Of course, the homestead and the stables were already here but it was his idea to train a few racehorses.'

'And made a success of it, too. Clive has a lot of respect for your father.'

Leila smiled, acknowledging the compliment although she was no particular fan of Clive Bannerman.

'So, where do you usually exercise around here? At Bannerman's we had a narrow sand track and also our own grass track forty metres wide and over two thousand metres long. There was also a pool for the horses to swim in.'

'No such luxuries here, I'm afraid. We do have a treadmill and a small sand track but otherwise we have to make use of what nature provides — the beach and the dunes. And of course we drive up to Cranbourne for trials. We meet the jockeys there.'

'Sounds good to me. Bluey has always loved swimming. But surely it's a bit chilly at this time of the year?' He was remembering the freezing temperature of the water the previous day.

'We use wet suits like the surfers, so we can go in the water all year round. I'd lend you Dad's but it would let in too much water — he's twice the size you are. There's a surf shop in Cowes where you can get kitted out — they do have second-hand ones if you don't want to buy new.'

'Thanks. I'll drive over later and get one.'

'I'll hitch a ride with you, if I may. I need to pick up some groceries, anyway.'

'Sure. But not till we've taken these two for a walk on the beach. Bluey didn't get enough exercise yesterday.'

Luckily, Bluey and Party Animal seemed to get along and they walked the horses quite a long way, chatting amicably of Bluey's spectacular wins and of mutual acquaintances in the racing industry.

'Jimmy,' she said at last. 'What will you do when Bluey retires? Surely, you're not going to stay with him when he's sent to stud?'

He frowned, looking uncomfortable. 'I don't know. I haven't thought about it.'

'Maybe you should,' she said gently. 'You know it must happen eventually and you won't even be thirty when it does — '

'Right now, Leila, I like to live in the present. Bluey still has a lot more to give.' He massaged away an incipient frown. 'I'm not a complete fool with my head in the sand — I know things can happen to horses, even champions. But I prefer to live in the present and take each day as it comes.' He gave her a tight smile.

'I'm sorry. I didn't mean to dig up things that upset you.'

'I'm not upset. I just don't like to think too far ahead, that's all.'

A silence fell between them then and Leila sighed. They had been getting on so well and her tactless queries had brought the barriers up again. She glanced at her watch. 'We haven't had lunch yet. We should be getting back if we want to drive over and catch the shops before they close,' she said. 'They don't stay open past five at this time of year.'

Back at the stables, Leila gave water to both of the horses and looked for some feed. She knew better than to offer anything to Bluey without checking with Jimmy first. Changing a horse's feed could cause serious illness like colic.

'What does he eat?' she asked. 'We must have one that he likes; we keep several varieties on hand.'

'Nothing but Graingers.' Jimmy showed her one of the bags he had brought with him, the familiar red and yellow logo on its side.

'Graingers?' Leila looked startled. 'But Jimmy, we can't afford Graingers. It's the most expensive food on the market. Pa says it's all hype, anyway. No better than anything else.'

'Sorry.' He shrugged. 'But at Bannerman's, apart from a bit of best quality hay from Clive's home farm, we never fed them anything else.'

Leila bit her lip. She was beginning to tire of hearing what happened at Bannerman's.

'Don't worry.' Jimmy grinned. 'It won't cost you a cent. Graingers have been sponsoring Bluey for years. They use him in their advertising. Surely, you've seen it?' He lowered his voice and adopted the stance of a TV presenter. '*A Champion's taste. The winning formula preferred by Starshine Blue. He never eats anything else*.' He returned to his normal voice. 'They send him a fresh supply every three months.'

'And whose idea was that?' Leila giggled, her good temper restored.

'Clive Bannerman's, of course. Who else?'

'And what if they stop providing it now that you've left?'

'Full of the *what ifs* today, aren't you?' Jimmy shrugged. 'If I have to, I'll buy it for him myself.'

It occurred to Leila yet again that Jimmy was no ordinary strapper but she kept that thought to herself.

Back at the house, she made some sandwiches for a quick, late lunch before they departed for the small, seaside town of Cowes.

Cowes was busy, even at this time of year. Since the island was home to many full-time residents and retirees, the shops were never left entirely alone. Leila pointed out the surf shop with boards propped outside and Jimmy parked outside it. As soon as he'd done so, Leila jumped down almost into the arms of a typical surfie with sun-streaked hair, wearing faded jeans and an old denim jacket.

'Leila!' he said, enfolding her in his embrace, clearly delighted to see her. 'What are you doing here? I didn't expect to see you in town today.'

'I didn't expect to come in myself but Jimmy here needs a wet suit.' Quickly she made the introductions. 'Our new foreman — Jimmy Flynn. Jimmy, this is Brett Hanson — my, er . . . '

'Nice to meet you, Jim.' Brett shook hands to cover for her stumbling introduction. He wasn't quite ready to let her call him her fiancé, not yet.

'Perhaps you could help him choose one while I'm at the supermarket?' she asked. 'Not the full thing with the mask and flippers — just a short one to cover the torso and keep him warm when we take the horses for a swim. I'll be back soon.' And without waiting for Brett's agreement, she turned away, crossing the road to go to the supermarket.

The two men stared after her, a little taken aback to be left so abruptly in each other's company.

'Be my guest,' Brett said at last. 'Do you want new or second hand?'

'New, I think.' Jimmy pulled a face. 'I don't like buying anyone else's trouble.'

'It's only a wet suit — not a car.' Brett grinned. 'But I know the bloke who owns the shop — he gives fifteen per cent to us locals and he'll probably give me a commission, if you're buying new.'

'Oh, Bre-ett!' A teenager, still in her school blazer and checked cotton uniform came sidling up to him, plucking his sleeve and making him close his eyes and wince. 'You promised to buy me coffee and said you'd take me to see that new film at the — '

'Not right now, Tanya,' he muttered through clenched teeth. 'Can't you see I'm busy? Anyway, Leila's here.'

'Oh, Leila!' The girl pouted, glaring in the direction of the supermarket. 'It isn't as if she owns you. Not yet.'

'Now Tanya, be a good girl and buzz off.' He gave her a playful slap on the bottom. 'I'll make it up to you later, I promise.'

'That's what you always say.' The girl's lip protruded still further but she gave him what she hoped was a sultry look from under her lashes.

'Kids!' Brett said to Jimmy as he stared after her, shaking his head.

'Yes, they can be a little demanding,' Jimmy said drily.

Once Tanya was gone, Brett was all business, helping Jimmy find the right wet suit and making sure it was a comfortable fit. If both he and the shop owner thought it surprising that Jimmy should use a gold credit card to pay for it, they didn't say anything. Jimmy shook hands with both of them and by the time he was ready to take his package to the car, Leila was back with her groceries.

'But you're not going home now, are you?' Brett said as she piled them into the back of the car and gave him a quick kiss on the cheek, preparing to leave. 'I was hoping you'd stay. We can have dinner out for once. Surely Jim can take the groceries home and I'll drop you off later?'

'I don't know.' She bit her lip, looking doubtful. 'I really ought to get back.'

'It's not a problem.' Jimmy smiled at her. 'I'm sure I can find my way home on my own.'

Brett slung an arm possessively across Leila's shoulders. ''Course you can. It's only a small place, after all. If you get lost, you can always ask.'

Jimmy saluted and drove off, watching them in the rearview mirror. With eyes only for each other, they didn't look back but, if they had, they would have seen the school-girl, lips trembling and eyes filled with incipient tears, watching from a shop doorway as they made slow progress down the street. He sighed, feeling sorry for Leila, who was being deceived, and also for the teenager who would feel such wounds sharply at her age. It was obvious that Brett, with that surfeit of boyish charm, twinkling blue eyes and happy-go-lucky ways, was a magnet for any number of girls. Although it was early days for him to make such a judgement, Jimmy decided he didn't like the guy, having him marked down as selfish and unable to remain faithful to any woman for any length of time.

Leila didn't come home until very late that night but Jimmy was still awake when she did. Tired as he was, sleep had evaded him and he squinted at the clock, seeing it was almost two when the reflection of a car's headlights swept around his bedroom walls. He heard a car door closing softly so as not to rouse the neighbourhood and the reflection of the head-lights backed off and moved swiftly away. He reminded himself that whatever Leila did, it wasn't his business, but he couldn't help feeling that she deserved better than Brett.

The following morning, he went across to the homestead and offered to cook fried eggs while Knud brewed coffee. There was no sign of Leila. Half an hour later, she appeared, looking wan, shuddering at the sight of food and refusing anything but a mug of black coffee, which she clasped between her hands as if she needed to keep warm.

'That's no way to start a working day,' her father complained. 'Brett should know better than to keep you out late when he knows you have to be up early in the morning.'

'Give it a rest, Pa,' Leila said. 'It's only once in a while.'

'Once too often so far as I'm concerned.'

Jimmy gave his attention to his food and kept silent. Although he hadn't known the Christensens for very long, he could tell it was unusual for them to be at odds with each other.

After breakfast, Jimmy and Leila took the horses down to the beach. This time they weren't alone as one of the other lads was working Dreamy Princess, who was being prepared for a country race meeting in about a week's time. The water was cold but the wet suit made a tremendous difference. The breeze had dropped and the ocean was calmer than it had been the previous day. Jimmy took Starshine Blue into the water to swim sideways against the waves. Enjoying his swim, the horse responded with vigour and all went well until Jimmy climbed down from his back to lead him ashore.

Bluey was startled by something under the water. It might not have been anything menacing — just the luminous scales of a fish catching the light or a crab scuttling for cover. He threw his head up unexpectedly and gave Jimmy a stunning blow to the chin. Leila saw it happen but didn't take a great deal of notice, expecting Jimmy to take it in his stride. Instead, he staggered out of the water and collapsed on the beach, his head in his hands.

'Can you take the other two horses back to the stables, Ben?' Leila diverted the lad who was gazing in astonishment at the fallen Jimmy. 'I'll look after Starshine Blue.'

'What's with him, then?' The lad nodded towards Jimmy. 'That's 'appened to me dozens of times. You wouldn't think he'd take it so hard.'

'I asked for your help, Ben. Not an opinion,' Leila said briskly. 'Please, just do as I ask and take the two horses back home.'

The lad shrugged and set off down the track towards Ocean's View, Party Animal and the mare walking meekly on either side of him.

Leila made sure she had hold of Bluey before approaching Jimmy who still hadn't moved from his position on the sands.

'Are you OK?' She said softly. 'I didn't realize he hit you that hard.'

'I'll be all right in a moment. Right now, I'm still seeing stars.'

'Is there anything I can do?'

'Not much.' He gave a shaky laugh. 'Apart from taking Bluey back to the stables for me.'

'Sure. But Jimmy, I don't like to leave you out here like this.'

'Honestly.' He tried to focus on her and give what he hoped was a reassuring smile. 'I just need to sit here a minute and catch my breath. I'll be fine.'

'Maybe I should come back with the car — '

'Good heavens, no. Ben's right. I shouldn't have to make such a fuss over a little bump on the head.'

'It wasn't Ben who took that bump on the head. I've had many a nose bleed for having my face in the wrong place at the right time. Bluey must've delivered a knock-out punch with his head.'

'I'm OK.' Jimmy lurched to his feet. 'Feeling better already.'

'I don't think so. You're still awfully white.'

'Come on. I'll help you get Bluey home.'

But as Jimmy took up a position on the other side of the horse, it occurred to her that he was actually leaning on Bluey, rather than leading the horse. All the same, by the time they reached the stables, Jimmy's colour had returned and he was himself again. He insisted on hosing down Starshine Blue himself and seeing to his feed. The vet was due in an hour or so to give all the Christensen horses a routine check-up.

3

Caulfield Racecourse was one of the more comfortable city courses in winter. Although there was room outside for those hardy enough to brave the wind which felt as if it was coming straight from the Antarctic, the races could be watched from stadium seating in the stands, under cover and behind glass. While Knud Christensen and his daughter went to the owners' and trainers' stand to meet and greet old friends, Jimmy walked Starshine Blue round to the stables to settle him in. He had been in fairly intensive training, had trialled well and was due to run in the fourth race of the day.

Jimmy was surprised to feel nervous and wondered if Bluey sensed it and felt the same. During the six years he had been with Clive Bannerman, he had never felt nervous on race days because when he started there, the horse was an unknown quantity with nothing to prove. Today he wanted him to do well for the Christensens and reassure them that Starshine Blue could still make it to the winners' circle where he belonged.

Although Jimmy would have preferred one

of the other lads to accompany him with Party Animal, who was also racing today, Bobby Johnson had insisted on sending Billy. It seemed the more time his son spent out of his sight, the better Johnson liked it. Party Animal was booked to run in race three, the one before Starshine Blue. Thinking of Billy somehow conjured him into view.

'Hey, Jimmy!' The lad stuck his head round from the neighbouring stall. 'Keep an eye on Party Animal, will ya? Jus' dropping out for a quick one.'

'Hang on, Bill. Can't you wait until after he's raced?' Jimmy started to say only to find himself talking to empty air. Without waiting for his permission, Billy had gone.

It wasn't easy for Jimmy to watch both horses. As a well-known champion, Bluey was exciting a fair amount of interest as people dropped by, either to assess his fitness or pay their respects.

'Are these the Christensen horses?' A skinny, young man addressed him and when he nodded, stepped forward to shake his hand, introducing himself.

'Simon Grant. I don't have any rides till race three with Party Animal, so I thought I'd come round and get acquainted.'

'And you're riding Bluey — Starshine Blue — in Race four, right?'

'Yeah. I ride a lot for the Christensens.' The boy smiled. 'They're good folks.'

They spent some time talking of horses and mutual acquaintance until Simon went off to get changed ready for race three. Jimmy glanced at his watch. Party Animal was due to be saddled and brought to the mounting yard but as yet Billy hadn't returned. He didn't want to seem like a dobber but if the lad didn't show up soon, the Christensens would have to be told. If he had to go up with Party Animal, he couldn't leave Starshine Blue unattended. Just as he was about to make the call, Leila Christensen arrived, solving the problem for him.

'I've just seen Billy Johnson reeling out of one of the bars,' she said, looking far from pleased. 'I'm so sorry, Jimmy. You've had to do everything.'

'Doesn't matter. I'm just glad you're here now.' He smiled at her in relief. 'I'll see to Party Animal, if you'll just stay here and mind Bluey.'

'It'll be a pleasure.' She traced the star with her finger and stroked the blue, velvety nose, then she patted his neck as the horse examined her with one wide, intelligent eye. All her earlier misgivings had melted away; she had fallen in love with the beautiful dark-blue horse.

Quickly and efficiently, Jimmy tacked up Party Animal, put on the corresponding numbered bib that Billy should have been wearing and led the animal out to the mounting yard. On the way, Billy came panting up after him.

'I'm supposed to do that. Why didn't you wait for me?'

'You're late, Bill. There's only ten minutes to the race.'

'Ah, to hell with you.' Billy was slurring his words. 'If you wanna make a big man of yourself an' do all the work on your own, why should I stop you?'

'You're drunk. Go and find somewhere to sleep it off.'

'Right. So you can go whining an' complainin' to ol' man Christensen? I don' think so.'

'I don't have to tell anyone anything, Bill. Leila saw you leaving the bar.'

'Ah yes, Leila,' Billy smirked, having trouble getting his tongue around his words. 'Lovely to look at but don' try to hold. Nothing doin' there, mate. She keeps her little trap door firmly closed.'

Ignoring Billy's drunken innuendos, Jimmy increased his pace until he reached the mounting yard where Knud and Simon were already waiting for him.

'Where's Billy?' Knud was quick to ask as Jimmy gave Simon a leg up into the saddle.

'It's OK,' Jimmy said. 'Leila's back there looking after Starshine Blue.'

'But she won't see the race. Party Animal is her horse.'

'There's still a minute or so to the jump. I could race back to the stables and let her come up. But you'll have to collect Party Animal from Simon when he comes back to scale.'

'Thanks, Jimmy. But Billy should be here, doing his job. This is the last time he comes to the city with me.'

'We'll discuss it later. Right now I want Leila to see her horse win,' Jimmy said with a smile, and was off.

Leila didn't lose any time returning to the stands. Sitting with Starshine Blue, Jimmy watched her make her way purposefully across the lawn, admiring her easy stride in spite of the high heels. He wondered what she would think of Bill Johnson's unsavoury remarks and decided he wouldn't want to be in Bill's shoes if she ever heard them.

Although he wasn't able to see the race from where he was seated, he could hear the commentary and winced as he heard a concerted gasp from the crowd at the onset of the race followed by a short pause in the commentary before it continued. Such things usually indicated an accident or a fall. He could only hope Party Animal wasn't involved, but now it was time to prepare Starshine Blue for his first city appearance for over a year.

Before he left for the mounting yard, a yawning, sheepish-looking Billy reappeared, leading Party Animal back to the stables.

'What a disaster,' he said. 'Didn't you hear? Party Animal knuckled on the way out of the gates and tipped Simon off.'

'Is he OK?'

'Simon or the horse?'

'Simon, of course. I can see the horse is OK.'

'Might have a broken arm. They've taken him off to hospital, anyway.'

'So who's going to ride Starshine Blue?'

'I dunno, do I?' Billy was getting impatient with all these questions. 'If you wanna know, you'd better get on up there and find out.'

At the mounting yard, as Jimmy walked around the circle, parading his horse, he could see no sign of the Christensens and assumed they would be doing their utmost to engage the services of another jockey. If no one was available, they'd have to scratch.

They reappeared at last, followed by a wizened gnome of a jockey wearing their colours of light and dark blue. Jimmy's heart sank as he recognized the jockey as Dave 'Stinger' Watkins — so named because of his fondness for using the whip.

'Jimmy.' Knud smiled, preparing to make introductions. 'This is — '

'Thanks. We've already met.' Jimmy glared at Watkins, his jaw set.

'Nice to see you again, too,' Watkins muttered as Knud assisted him into the saddle to take charge of the horse. He could see that Jimmy wasn't about to do the honours. 'Well now, Bluey,' he talked to the horse as he adjusted his feet into the stirrups. 'Are we going to see eye to eye today?'

The horse flattened his ears and snorted as Watkins trotted him away and gave him a sharp taste of the whip to urge him into a canter as they reached the track.

Jimmy sighed, watching them. 'I wish you'd hired anyone but Dave Watkins.'

'So do I,' Leila chimed in. 'Honestly, Pa. What were you thinking?'

'He was the only jockey available, Leila.' Knud was for once less than affable. 'Would you prefer to see him scratched and go home empty-handed?'

'Yes. I think I would.' Leila was close to tears. 'Anyone could see the horse didn't like him.' Having a sudden thought, she turned to

Jimmy. 'You don't like him either, do you? He's ridden Bluey before?'

'Not for some time. But unfortunately Bluey remembers him.'

'There you are, Pa. I told you we should have cleared it with Jimmy before letting Watkins take him.'

'He was the only jockey available and we were running out of time,' Knud persisted as they made their way back to the stands to watch the race. 'All we can do now is sit tight an' keep our fingers crossed.'

'A lot can happen over two thousand metres,' Jimmy muttered, trying to identify Bluey among the horses assembling behind the barriers. It was quite a large field.

'You're worried about him, aren't you?' Leila whispered, surprising him by taking his hand. Hers felt small and cold in his own.

Jimmy nodded although he attempted a reassuring smile. There was no time for further conversation as the barriers flew open and the field was on its way.

They passed the winning post for the first time without event, the field moving at an even pace with no one pushing to take the lead at this stage. They identified Watkins who had Starshine Blue on the fence about midfield.

'No and no!' Jimmy was groaning under his

breath. 'If there's anything Bluey hates, it's being hemmed in and surrounded on all sides. He likes to set his own pace and needs plenty of room.'

The field jogged along, each horse holding his position as they moved away from the stands, progressing around the far side of the track.

'No change in the order,' the race caller was having difficulty getting any sense of excitement into the race. 'Pinkerton still in the lead, closely followed by Black Rose but this is more like it. They've quickened the pace and are coming away from the fence, starting to bunch as they reach the home turn. And here he comes. Here comes Starshine Blue with Dave Watkins, practically jumping out of the saddle, urging the horse to give his all. What did I tell you? You can't keep a champion down. Black Rose is gone, Pinkerton holds on for second place but Starshine Blue — Starshine Blue and Dave Watkins have won by five lengths.'

'Yes!' Knud punched the air. 'I knew he could do it.'

But Leila exchanged a glance with Jimmy and she wasn't smiling. While people crowded around to congratulate Knud, she and Jimmy raced down to the winners' enclosure where Watkins would have to dismount.

‘See that?’ Watkins was on a high as he greeted them, sliding to the ground before retrieving his saddle. ‘I made him run. I put some salt on his tail.’ He was too pleased with himself to see that Jimmy and Leila weren’t smiling.

Bluey still had his ears back and was blowing hard as he fought to recover his breath. Leila took the reins, patting his neck and soothing the trembling animal while Jimmy, white with fury, went to examine his haunches to see what damage had been done. It didn’t take long. The evidence was there for all to see.

‘You bastard! You hit him so hard you’ve almost broken the skin.’

‘Well, he’s an’ old un, isn’t he?’ Dave was starting to whine. ‘I had to belt the hell out of him. Only way to get him to lift his game an’ get past the post.’

Jimmy had heard enough and his temper snapped. As Dave put his nose in the air and turned to leave, annoyed that he hadn’t received the praise he expected, Jimmy snatched the jockey’s whip from his hand and gave him two smart cracks across the shoulders. ‘See how *you* like it,’ he said through gritted teeth.

Dave yelped — more in surprise than pain — as Jimmy threw the whip to the ground. If he could have snapped it in two, he would have done so. As it was, with his arms already filled with his saddle, the jockey had to bend and scrabble for it in the mud. People glanced at each other, having heard Dave's shout, but the incident was over so quickly, nobody saw what had happened.

'You'll pay for that, Jimmy Flynn,' he muttered. 'Don't think you've heard the last of it.'

'You haven't, either,' Jimmy said, still shaking with fury. 'I'm going to report you for excessive and abusive use of the whip.'

'Go to hell. You get above yourself, Jimmy Flynn. You're not the owner or trainer of that horse.' He then addressed himself to Leila: 'Your Dad wanted me to make the horse win an' I did. End of story.' With a sarcastic salute to Leila, he gave Jimmy a last, hard stare.

'Horrible man. Pa should never have hired him.' Leila shook her head, watching the jockey stamp off to weigh in. 'Everyone knows what he's like.'

Gradually, the horse was recovering now he'd had a drink and realized he was back in safe hands. Jimmy took the precaution of showing his injury to the veterinary officer on course who agreed to endorse his complaint against Watkins and gave them an antibiotic salve to put on the horse's injuries. Having no further involvement in the races that day, they boxed the two horses and prepared to go home, knowing there was still a long drive ahead of them to the coast.

'If you don't mind riding home with Jimmy, I'll get him to give you a lift,' Knud said to Leila. 'I've told Bill Johnson I want him to ride home with me. I need to have a serious conversation with that young man and I don't want to pull any punches because you're there.'

'Oh dear.' Leila's face fell. 'We've won a major race and it ought to have been a happy day. Somehow it hasn't turned out that way.' She sighed, not wanting to tell her father about the incident between Jimmy and Watkins. Not right now, anyway, when he had other things on his mind. Maybe she would confide in him later when they were home.

She helped Jimmy to secure the two horses in their box and climbed up into the passenger seat of his Toyota. In spite of its owner's occupation the car was immaculate inside with no dirt or mud and still smelling of new leather. Sighing with contentment, Leila fastened herself into the comfortable, well sprung seat at his side.

'This is a lovely car, Jimmy,' she couldn't help remarking as he drove carefully from the course so as not to shake up the horses. 'Have you had it long?'

'Only since March. It was a twenty-fifth birthday present.'

'Wow! You must have a very rich uncle.'

'No. It came from Clive Bannerman.'

'Really?' She gave a wry smile. 'I hope you're not hoping for birthday presents like that from Pa,' she said, thinking of their own battered Range Rover which her father was now driving home.

'It wasn't all that expensive — just a practical car for everyday use.'

'Still looks like top of the range to me.'

Thinking she implied that he didn't deserve it, Jimmy felt the need to justify his position.

'During the six years we were with Clive, Bluey earned more than two million in prize money. And if you must know, the car was more than a birthday present, it was also a bribe, an inducement to stay. Clive wanted me to be first assistant to the stable foreman — to take charge when the main man wasn't there.'

She stared at him, amazed at this revelation. 'Jimmy, you must be crazy. You turned your back on an offer like that to come to a small operation like ours?'

He shrugged. 'I've had tempting offers

before.' He was thinking of his refusal to join his father's business empire. 'And I'd still rather be a big fish in a smaller pond. Your father was prepared to give Bluey a chance when Clive had lost faith in him. Far as I'm concerned, the choice I made was the right one — for Bluey and for me.'

'But with a job like that you would have been set for life.'

'Not necessarily. Clive runs his show rather like the court of a medieval king — he plays new favourites all the time.' He felt uncomfortable, well aware that he was telling her only half the truth. He didn't say that Clive gave him the car as a sweetener when he sustained a bad fall during track work — partly his own fault for not wearing proper protective headgear. To avoid paying a higher premium for his already substantial work cover insurance, Clive met all his medical expenses including a check-up with a neurosurgeon and an opthalmologist. Initially he had suffered blurred vision followed by headaches. Occasionally, when he was over-tired, he had them still but he didn't mention that either. He was hoping that Leila had forgotten the incident at the beach.

'Knowing Clive, I'm surprised he didn't want the car back when you didn't take up his offer,' Leila said, intruding on his thoughts.

'No. He said I could keep it.' He shrugged, unable to meet her candid gaze and keeping his eyes on the road. 'He'd have written it off as a business expense, anyway.'

Conversation lapsed briefly as they took the highway that would take them a lot of the way towards home.

'Do you have family, Jimmy?' she said at last.

'Yes, but we're not that close. My mum died when I was fourteen and I don't see eye to eye with my Dad. I do have a sister who's nine years older than me but as we didn't really grow up together, she's more like a young aunt. She has the head for business that I don't. I'm sure my father would have preferred it if she'd been the boy of the family and not me.' He checked himself, not wanting to reveal too much more.

'It's a shame you're not close.' Leila's expression clouded. 'Family is important.' She was thinking of the good relationship she had with her own father. 'Your dad is in business, you say?'

Jimmy almost flinched, thinking that his carefree days as a strapper would soon be over if Leila and Knud were to find out that he was an heir to the Kirkwood millions. 'Just say we lead very different lives. Can we leave it at that, please?' He switched on the radio and changed stations until he found one devoted to country music and turned up the volume, making conversation impossible.

Leila studied his profile, wishing she had the skill to be tactful. Her father was always telling her she was too direct, too intrusive. Now Jimmy had clammed up and she would get nothing more. During this long journey, taking several hours, she had hoped to find out more about Jimmy Flynn. He had been at Ocean's View for over two months now and although his work was more than satisfactory and he was undoubtedly an asset to the stables, they didn't know any more about him than they did when he arrived. Knud was too trusting, she knew. Tempted by the offer to take on this ageing champion, he had accepted Jimmy without even seeing him, agreeing to make him stable foreman as well. But from Jimmy's guarded attitude and reluctance to talk about his family or background, she could only assume he must have something to hide.

As they approached the small settlement of San Remo before crossing the bridge to Phillip Island, she turned down the music and spoke to him.

'There's a café over there on the left and a loading zone where you can pull up for a moment. I'll get us some coffee.'

'Thanks,' he said, grateful that the tension between them seemed to have evaporated. He knew he had been short with her and was relieved that she didn't seem to expect an apology or bear a grudge.

She returned moments later with two polystyrene cups. 'I hate these things but we can't sit inside and leave the horses unattended.'

'That's OK. Thanks.' He accepted one of the cups and sipped the coffee cautiously. It was scalding.

'I'm so sorry, Jimmy. I didn't mean to pry. My Pa's always telling me how tactless I am.'

'It's OK.' He shrugged. 'But there's really not much to know. I'm a very uninteresting person, really.'

Leila gave him a sidelong glance. She didn't find him uninteresting at all with those long-lashed dark brown eyes and shock of dark hair that invited the touch of a woman's hand. And his secrecy only made him all the more intriguing.

Back at Ocean's View, Leila saw that her father's car was already parked under the pergola alongside the house. And there was another behind it. Brett Hanson's station wagon, his surf boards on the roof rack. Without waiting for her to jump down from Jimmy's vehicle and come into the house, he came out to greet her, hands on hips.

'About time, Leila,' he said. 'Where have you been, skiving off with the hired help? Your father got back more than half an hour ago.'

'Well, Brett.' She took her time getting out of the car before looking him up and down, clearly unimpressed and putting Jimmy in mind once again of an icy Nordic princess. 'Since we parted bad friends the last time we met, I wasn't expecting to see you — tonight or any other night.' She turned to Jimmy, patting the bonnet of the Toyota. 'Lovely ride, Jimmy. Thanks for bringing me home.' Deliberately, she was drawing Brett's attention to the Toyota, comparing it with his rusty, salt-stained Holden that smelled of seaweed and more often than not had damp wet suits hanging inside. Jimmy gave her a jaunty salute and nodded to Brett as he turned the car and the horsebox towards the stables. Brett didn't even acknowledge it.

'Come on, Leila,' he said, catching a tendril of her hair and pulling it none too gently. 'Don't be like that. You know we always kiss and make up. We're supposed to go to the Thompsons' barbecue tonight,' he said. 'Or had you forgotten?'

'No. But you've forgotten I said we were finished and I didn't want to see you again.'

'Yes, but you didn't mean it.'

'Didn't I? Honestly, Brett — Tanya Hopkins? A child, a schoolgirl, not even sixteen.'

'I didn't know.' He spread his hands, looking injured. 'She said she was eighteen. Seemed to know exactly what she was doing, too.'

'Spare me the details, Brett.'

'Come on, Leila. Tanya means nothing — she's just a kid.' As she continued to gaze at him, still frosty, he gave her the wide smile that usually brought him all that he wanted, his teeth perfect, white against his seasoned tan. 'Change into something warm and casual and lets get going. The party must have started an hour ago.'

'Can't I go as I am?' She looked down at her best turquoise suit and high heels.

'I don't think so. You look like the Queen.'

'All right. But only because the Thompsons are new neighbours and I don't want to let them down.' She hurried towards the stairs and then paused, remembering she hadn't left Knud anything for his supper. Nor had she asked him what happened with Billy. She started towards the kitchen but Knud forestalled her.

'Leila, go,' he said, seeing her hesitation. 'It's Saturday night. You should be enjoying yourself, not worrying about the old man.

I've got plenty of beer, there's a pie in the fridge and I won't mind my own company for once — I'll be able to watch the footie.'

'You sound as if you want to get rid of me!'

'I do.' Her father nodded, grinning. 'I want to watch the semi-final without you groaning and asking to change the channel.'

Upstairs she put on a new pair of jeans and black boots, adding a figure-hugging black sweater with a plunging neckline. Thinking the neckline too provocative when she was still angry with Brett, she added a silk scarf to hide it. She brushed her hair into a shining fall and secured it on one side with a diamante hairclip, allowing the other side to fall forward. She renewed her make-up, added a spray of her favourite Givenchy perfume, blew herself a kiss in the mirror and was ready to go.

'I say,' Brett murmured appreciatively. 'You always brush up so well.' He went to kiss her but she ducked under his arm, avoiding it.

'Don't wait up for me, Pa.' She gave Knud a swift kiss on the cheek instead.

'And don't you stay out too late,' her father warned. 'There's still the same amount of work to do in the morning.'

4

The Thompsons were fairly close neighbours, having a property right on a cliff overlooking the beach. Very much a seaside house, built to take advantage of the magnificent views on all sides, it had always been a bit of a show place, having been built some time in the prosperous eighties by a rock star, now busy consolidating a career in LA. Having driven past the high fence that surrounded it every time she left Ocean's View to take the road to town, Leila had never seen inside it and was unlikely to do so today. The Thompsons were determined to keep their daughter's eighteenth birthday party 'alfresco'.

The patio was ablaze with lights, including a string of pretty Chinese lanterns and people were already dancing to a small band, playing on a stage erected on the beach. An open tent stood alongside, containing the bar. It had all the appearances of a summer party although it was only early September and the evening was cool. On one side of the patio was a blazing fire in a Mexican chiminea pizza oven although most people were standing around it just to keep warm. On the other side, just above the steps leading down to the beach, two gas barbecues were sizzling away, one to grill sausages, steak and chops for the carnivores and the other roasting prawns in a sauce of garlic and chilli as well as slices of eggplant and other vegetarian options. Leila's stomach rumbled. Apart from a sandwich, eaten quickly on the way to the track, she'd had nothing to eat all day.

'Don't let's bother with food now, I'd rather have a beer,' Brett murmured into her neck before looking up to smile and wave at his surfie friends already clustered around the bar. Leila could see Bill Johnson among them and hesitated, not wanting to meet up with him. He had been well on the way to being drunk at the races and now he was looking red-faced and belligerent, ready to pick a fight.

'I don't want to drink on an empty stomach,' she said. 'And those prawns do smell delicious.'

'Go and eat then, if you must.' Brett shoved her none too gently in the direction of the barbecue, giving her the impression he thought she was greedy. 'I'll spend some time with the lads and catch you later when you've eaten your fill.' And without waiting for her reply, he left, pushing his way through the crowd to join his friends at the bar.

Leila stared after him, equally irritated. Tired and hungry after their eventful day at the races, she would much prefer to have stayed at home. Brett had insisted on making her join the party, only to desert her as soon as they arrived.

She found a paper plate, some bread and butter and attached herself to the small crowd waiting for the next batch of prawns, accepting a delicious slice of roasted capsicum while they cooked. They wouldn't take long. She glanced around, surprised to see so many people she didn't know and feeling suddenly shy. Of course the Thompsons were new neighbours and Jenny, their daughter, was several years younger than she was. Most of their friends would have come from town. She could see Jenny now, dressed in a glittering pink top over skintight jeans and shaking her expensively straightened blonde hair down her back. Jenny spotted her at the same time, greeting her with a teenage shriek of joy.

'Leila! Glad you could make it.' She looked past her, suddenly anxious. 'Isn't Brett with you? He promised me he would come?'

'He's here all right.' Leila tried hard to keep the exasperation from her voice. 'Over there with his friends at the bar.'

'Oh Brett! Brett!' Jenny screamed. Leila

watched the exuberant teenager run towards him and hurl herself into his arms. Laughing, Brett lifted her off her feet and whirled her around as she rested her hands on his shoulders, smiling down at him. Leila turned away so as not to see the inevitable kiss and wondered why Brett had troubled to bring her with him at all. By now, he was probably wondering the same thing. All his surfie friends were here and Jenny was transparently anxious to replace her as his girlfriend. Perhaps he just wanted to humiliate her and make her suffer a little for saying she didn't want to see him any more.

The prawns were being distributed and she accepted three on her plate, looking for somewhere to sit down and eat them.

'Would you like to share my rock?' a voice said close beside her, making her jump. 'Sorry, didn't mean to scare you.'

'Jimmy Flynn!' She said, genuinely pleased to see him. 'What are you doing here?'

'Believe it or not,' he said. 'Much as I love Bluey, I'm not tied to his apron strings — or his saddle. Occasionally, I do step out and have a life of my own.' He made room for her beside the flat rock supporting his own meal of roasted vegetables and bread.

'I'm sorry.' She felt herself blush and was grateful for the gathering darkness. 'I've done it again, haven't I? I didn't mean to make it sound as if you shouldn't be here.'

'Just eat, woman,' he murmured, his mouth full. 'If you've had as little as I have today, you'll be starving.'

'I am. Thanks,' she said, giving her full attention to the delicious food on her plate. She mopped up the juices with her bread and sighed with contentment when she finished.

'More?' he said. 'Yours looked so good, I'm going to try them. Stay here and I'll get some for both of us.'

Happy to do as he asked, she sat watching the stars. It was a clear night and they were shining brightly enough to light up the night. A peal of laughter made her look towards the scantily dressed teenagers dancing on the beach, oblivious to the cool breeze coming off the sea. She squinted to look at her watch and saw it was already after ten; the time she was usually in bed and asleep. She stifled a yawn and glanced in the direction of the bar but could see no sign of Brett although she recognized some of his friends among the dancers on the beach.

Seeing Jimmy on his way back with two steaming plates of prawns, she stood up, ready to take one. But before she could do so or even cry out to warn him, Bill Johnson stuck out a leg to trip him up, laughing as

Jimmy stumbled, sending prawns and bread flying in all directions to be ruined in the sand. Jimmy himself fell awkwardly, bruising his nose on a rock.

'I saw you, Bill Johnson!' Leila said. 'You did that on purpose.'

'Too right, I did.' Johnson was smirking and waving a can of beer aloft. 'I don't have to pretend to like any of you any more. I suppose you know your father gave me the sack?'

'No, I didn't,' Leila said slowly, knowing that Knud would only have done so if he had no alternative; as a rule, he avoided unpleasantness of any sort, letting people take advantage of his good nature. 'I'm sure he didn't want to. If only you could have mended your ways and met him halfway . . .'

'Mended my ways?' Bill almost snorted. 'What for? There wasn't much of a job left for me, was there? Not after you brought *him* in over our heads.' He shot a glance towards Jimmy who was being assisted back on to his feet while someone beat the sand from his clothes. Someone else had offered a handful of paper napkins to stem the bleeding from his nose. Seeing there was an altercation with Leila at the centre of it, Brett pushed his way through the gathering crowd to reach her side.

'Leave you alone for five minutes and you get into trouble,' he teased. 'What's going on here?'

'Nothing,' she said. 'Just Billy Johnson showing off his good manners as usual.'

'That's not so surprising.' Brett shrugged. 'Since he reckons your friend there got him the sack.' He jerked his head towards Jimmy. 'Come on, let them get on with it if they want a scrap. Let's go and dance.'

'No, thanks.' Like a matador, she twirled aside, avoiding him.

'Ah, Leila, don't be like that. I thought we'd kissed and made up?'

'No Brett, not this time and not any more.' She spoke softly but with determination. Having taken the time to collect her thoughts, she knew what she wanted now. 'I'm tired of being your doormat.'

'But you're not. Really, you're not.'

'No? Listen to what you say to me about kissing and making up. Until now I've let you, haven't I? You were the centre of my universe and I thought I couldn't live without you but I'm finding I can.' The last sentence came out in a rush of relief. 'The whole thing's gone stale. I can't do this any more.'

'Leila, please. You don't mean it — '

'Yes.' Steadily, she met his gaze. 'This time I do. You can't help it, Brett — it's not even your fault, it's the way you are. I grew up and you didn't — it's as simple as that.'

'But, Leila, I love you. We're meant for each other.'

'No. I'm just a bad habit you're used to, that's all.'

Brett swayed on his feet, breathing heavily as he tried to digest her words. 'So, you're giving me marching orders, are you?' He glared around belligerently. 'Who has done this? Who's stolen you from me?'

'Nobody. There is no one else. I just need some space, some time on my own, right now.'

Unaware of the drama that had been taking place between them, Jenny Thompson came running up from the beach to hurl herself into Brett's arms and gaze adoringly into his eyes. 'Dance with me, Brett.' She smiled at him, pouting prettily. Clearly, this was something that had served her well since she was a child. 'It's my party and I'm the princess for the night. Everyone has to do as I say.'

'Yes. Go and dance with her, Brett.' Leila spoke so softly that only he would hear. 'And please try to treat her better than you did me.'

Bemused, he blinked at Leila and smiled hesitantly at Jenny, allowing her to draw him away. Leila stared after him, tears suddenly pricking her eyes. She had made the right decision, she was sure of it. But watching

Brett leave, his arm resting casually across Jenny's shoulders, felt like saying goodbye to her own teenage years.

As soon as they realized the argument had petered out and there was to be no fighting, the party guests lost interest and dispersed, some returning to dance to the band, now striking up with some lively disco tunes, while others went to quench their thirst at the bar. Leila and Jimmy found themselves left on the fringes of the party like flotsam washed up on the beach.

'Are you OK?' he said from where he was sitting on their rock, the blood in his nose making him sound as if he had a cold. He was perhaps the only witness to her final break-up with Brett.

'Never felt better.' She smiled bravely. 'I should have done that a long time ago. But, more importantly, how are you?' she said, crouching beside him. 'You've gone awfully white. Like you did at the beach that day.'

'Thanks.' He laughed shortly.

'I don't feel like eating anything now, do you?'

'Uhuh.' He shook his head and then winced, realizing he shouldn't have done that as it made him feel dizzy. Shakily, he tried to stand, only to stumble and sit down heavily again.

'That stupid Billy. He really hurt you,

didn't he? I could kill him for this.'

Jimmy smiled grimly. 'It isn't entirely Bill's fault. He wouldn't have known.'

'Known what?' she asked, feeling more than a little anxious.

'All right. You've seen me in trouble twice, so I might as well come clean and tell you. I fell off a horse during track work at Bannerman's — and no, it wasn't Bluey — I fell on my head and it must have affected my eyesight. Everyone expected it to be temporary. But now, if I fall or sustain any kind of blow to the head, I feel dizzy and see double for a couple of hours. It's nothing to worry about, really. It wears off when I've had a bit of a rest.'

'But Jimmy, that's serious. Eyesight is precious. You should see someone about this.'

'I already have. They advised me not to get into fights or get bumped on the head.'

'And to steer clear of the Bill Johnsons of this world,' she said with a wry smile.

'Well, yes. Leila, I hate to trouble you but can you get me into the car and drive us home? If anyone sees me like this, they're going to say I'm drunk.'

'They'd better not say so to me.' She gazed around fiercely, challenging anyone to speak as Jimmy eased himself to a standing position and took a deep breath.

'Can you see where you're going at all?' she asked, supporting him around the waist, surprised to find how natural and comfortable it felt. He smelled wonderful, too; of hay and some subtle, expensive cologne. For the second time, it crossed her mind that this was no ordinary strapper.

'Yeah, but my balance has gone.' He laughed weakly. 'The world keeps tilting to one side.'

'Best if we don't go upstairs to say our goodbyes, then.' She let him lean on her and he didn't weigh heavily; for a tall man, he was very slender. 'We'll go the long way round. Where's your car?' she muttered, glancing towards the road. 'It's OK — I've spotted it. Good job you parked there instead of outside the house with the others.'

'Didn't want to get bailed up. Leila, are you sure you're OK to drive the Prado? I'll never make it.'

'Can I drive the Prado!' She pretended to be offended. 'I'll have you know I've a full licence to drive a horse float. Of course I can drive that little beach buggy of yours.'

'Beach buggy?'

'Only teasing.' She took the keys from him, unlocked the car and helped him up into the passenger seat where he leaned back breathing deeply for a moment with closed eyes. 'Does the dizziness make you feel sick?'

'No,' he lied. 'I'll be all right in a moment.'

'You don't want me to take you to a hospital?'

'No, thanks. Even the thought of going there makes me feel worse.'

Leila went round and climbed into the driver's seat. In truth she wasn't quite as confident of driving his car as she said. It was a powerful vehicle, she didn't want to be responsible for the smallest scratch. Fortunately, she didn't have to drive far and was soon parking outside the Johnsons' cottage. She jumped down and went round to help him get out. Jimmy managed to climb down but felt giddy again and had to sit down heavily on the front steps of the cottage, his head in his hands as he tried to stop the world spinning around him.

'Oh my lord — he's not drunk, is he?' Myrtle Johnson had heard them arrive and was now standing in the doorway watching them, her voice heavy with disapproval. 'He can sleep it off in the stables if he's going to be sick.'

'Jimmy's not drunk but your son was.' Leila was infuriated by the woman's unsympathetic attitude. 'He stuck out his leg and tripped Jimmy up.'

'My Bill? Never.' She sniffed with indignation. 'Nobody ever has a good word to say for him but I know my boy. He wouldn't have meant any harm. Even if that one did carry tales to your father.' She gave Jimmy a scathing glance. 'Got my poor Billy the sack, he did.'

'Myrtle, what's up?' Bob Johnson loomed in the doorway behind her in pyjamas and dressing gown, his eyes heavy with sleep. 'You're making enough noise down here to waken the dead.'

'More false accusations against our Bill,' Myrtle announced, folding her arms and glaring at Leila. As they were leaving in a matter of days, she could see no reason to ingratiate herself now.

'Bill was drunk at the races — I saw him myself,' Leila said. 'And he was drinking again with Brett at the party.'

'And why shouldn't he drown his sorrows, poor lamb, after getting the sack?' Myrtle sniffed again.

'Poor lamb?' Bob Johnson was awake now and ready to join the argument. 'I'd say it's no more than he deserved. Bill had every opportunity to prove his worth here and he blew it.'

'An unnatural father, that's what you are!' Myrtle rounded on him. 'You've never stood up for him or supported him . . . '

'Excuse me,' Leila broke in. She'd heard

enough of the Johnsons' domestic argument for one night. 'But Jimmy's the injured party here and he needs to get to bed.'

'I can look after him now, Miss Christensen.' Myrtle assumed a martyred air. 'You needn't wait.'

'Thank you, Mrs Johnson.' Leila returned her formality. 'But I won't keep you from your bed. I'll make sure Jimmy's comfortable before I leave. We may need to call a doctor or drive him to the hospital if he isn't better in the morning.' She extended a hand to Jimmy and hauled him to his feet. 'Upstairs on the right, isn't it?'

'Leila, I'll be OK,' he protested feebly. 'You don't have to come up.'

She ignored him, placing her arm firmly around him as she led him towards the stairs. 'Show's over, folks — g'night,' she said, dismissing the Johnsons. Myrtle opened her mouth to say something more and decided against it, pursing her lips with disapproval instead.

The room Jimmy occupied was sparsely decorated with the exception of a dozen or so photographs, commemorating the many triumphs of Starshine Blue. No family photos but, from the little he had confided, she knew there weren't likely to be. He seemed to have no life at all outside his connection with this particular horse. The walls of the cottage were thin and she could hear the Johnsons continuing their argument in the room across the hall. She sighed, wondering if all marriages must end with domestic arguments over children, grown up or not.

She helped him out of his black leather jacket and, gratefully, Jimmy sighed and stretched out fully clothed on his bed. As he did so, she saw that something of his natural tan had returned; there was no longer the same waxy pallor. She pulled off his boots and saw they were of the very best quality just like the jacket. *Who are you, Jimmy Flynn?* she asked herself. *Certainly not the itinerant gypsy you'd have us believe.*

She eased him out of his shirt, intending to let him sleep in his singlet and underpants, and he sighed with contentment, already half asleep. But when she went to unbuckle his trousers, he laughed softly, trapping her hands in his own to prevent her.

'No, Dianne, you naughty girl,' he murmured. 'You mustn't do that.'

Leila backed away from the bed as if she had been stung. What a fool she'd been to think he was a man alone, devoted only to his horse. Of course he must have a girlfriend — a girlfriend whose name was Dianne. He was probably only waiting for the Johnsons to leave before he brought her to Ocean's View.

And what had she been thinking herself? Vulnerable in the face of Brett's constant betrayals, unconsciously had she cast Jimmy in the role of taking his place? Back by the bed and unable to resist it, she ruffled his hair, soft and springy to the touch and then rolled the bedclothes around the man who had already given himself up to sleep. He had never been hers, not even for a moment, but mentally she returned him to his Dianne, whoever she might be.

Glancing towards the chest of drawers opposite the bed — the only other piece of furniture in the room — she considered taking a quick look through it to see if she could gain any further insight into the mystery that was Jimmy Flynn. He stirred on the bed, murmuring in his sleep, and she decided against it. She would have no excuse to offer if he awoke to find her going through his private papers and other belongings. Glancing at her watch, she stifled a yawn, surprised to see it was only ten past eleven. The last hour had been so eventful, it felt as if it were the early hours of the morning.

'Jimmy,' she whispered, not really expecting a reply. 'Is there anything else you need?'

He sat up suddenly, surprising her by looking at her as if he could see her clearly. 'I called you Dianne.'

'Yes,' she said. 'But it doesn't matter. I was only trying to make you comfortable so you could sleep. We can send for Dianne to come and look after you tomorrow . . . '

'Send for Dianne? God forbid.' He shuddered. 'That would be the last thing I'd want.'

'Oh? I thought — '

'Please, Leila, don't try to think for me. I'll be OK in the morning. In fact, after closing my eyes and letting the world stop spinning, I feel a lot better now.'

'Well, don't get up too early. We can manage without you, for once.'

'Can you? You'll be short-handed without Bill Johnson!'

'For the amount of work Bill Johnson did, he might as well not have been there.'

'Yes but Bluey will — '

'Don't you worry about Bluey. I'll look after him for you myself.'

'Yes, but you know what he's like.' Jimmy chewed his lip. 'He won't eat properly if I'm not there.'

'Then he can learn to get over himself. We can't have him behaving like a spoilt brat.'

'But he *is* a spoilt brat,' Jimmy laughed. 'It's his thing.'

They both jumped at a sudden, insistent

knocking at the bedroom door. It opened an inch or two to show Myrtle Johnson's nose and suspicious eyes.

'Miss Christensen!' She sniffed, anxious to uphold the morals in her house. 'There's been a lot of giggling going on in here. And if Jimmy's feeling better, I think it's time you left.'

'You're right, of course, Mrs Johnson,' Leila said breezily. 'Too much giggling can't be good for anyone, can it?' She gave Jimmy a cheeky wink which was really more for Mrs Johnson's benefit than his. 'See you in the morning, Jim.'

5

It was after midnight by the time Leila wearily climbed the stairs, longing for bed, her head spinning with the events of the day. There were no lights on in the living room nor any sound from the TV so she knew the football match must be over and her father already in bed. She wouldn't disturb him; there would be plenty of time to catch up in the morning. Easygoing as he was, she knew he wouldn't have liked the task of sacking Bill Johnson. Far from being grateful to be free of a job that held no interest for him, the lad seemed bitter and resentful about his dismissal. His parents were due to leave any day now and Leila could only hope he'd choose to go with them to make a new life up North, even if he wasn't welcome in his uncle's house.

Tired as she was, sleep didn't come easily and she found herself thinking of Brett. Maybe he did love her — so far as he was capable of loving anyone — but every time a new girl arrived on the scene, he couldn't resist it. He had to try his luck and give chase. While they were still at school it hadn't mattered so much but now she was older, she wanted a proper relationship — a real commitment from someone she could trust.

Against her better judgment, she had been sleeping with Brett for several years but even that made no difference to his roving ways. No. If anything, he had taken her even more for granted. It was definitely the right thing to do to cut her losses and end it.

Finally, her thoughts turned towards Jimmy, that intriguing man of mystery. Although nothing further than banter had passed between them, she sensed that there could be more and that he did, too. When he thought she wasn't aware of it, he watched her intently and she couldn't deny the undertow of attraction that drew her towards him. Even so, she warned herself, she should be wary of getting too close to anyone right now, in case she was on the rebound from Brett. It would be foolish to jump into a new relationship, particularly with someone like Jimmy with whom she was working so closely. If things didn't work out, it would be hard to maintain a professional relationship. All the same, before drifting into sleep, she allowed herself the small luxury of wondering if Jimmy Flynn was a good kisser and even how it might feel to lie in the safety of his embrace. Sighing contentedly, she fell asleep with a smile on her lips.

In the morning, when the alarm went off, she remembered the events of the previous night and waited for the familiar wave of melancholy to wash over her as it usually did when she quarrelled with Brett. Instead, she felt a surge of elation, like a wild bird finding itself unexpectedly released from a cage. The sense of renewed freedom made her almost light-headed. Brett was no longer a part of her life and she didn't have to worry about him any more. She showered, singing, and put on a bright red shirt along with her work clothes, to echo her mood.

'What did you do? Win the lottery?' Knud said as he ladled a generous amount of porridge into a bowl for her. 'Or has Brett come up with the engagement ring at long last?'

'Brett's gone, Pa.' She saw no point in pretending otherwise. 'I gave him my blessing and sent him off into the sunset — or rather into the arms of Jenny Thompson.' She considered this for a moment. 'Although I don't know if I've done the poor girl any favours. I hope it isn't something she'll live to regret.'

Knud peered at her over his spectacles. 'But Leila, are you sure? You and Brett have been together for more than five years now.'

'Not really together — not as we ought to have been. I was trying not to face up to it and that's why we lasted so long but he's a womanizer, Pa. I'm tired of making excuses for him, pretending not to see.'

'Well, I can't say I'm sorry to hear it. I never thought he was good enough for you, anyway.'

'Oh, Pa.' She gave him a wry smile. 'That's what all fathers say.'

'No. I'm happy to see you've come to your senses. I knew he'd make you miserable in the end.'

She stared at him in surprise. 'But why didn't you say so? You never told me you didn't like him.'

'What would have been the point? You thought the sun and the moon shone out of those cruel blue eyes. Criticism from me would only have fanned the flames. You would have resented it, turning your back on me.'

'Oh, Pa.' She got up from the breakfast table and went to hug him where he was seated, putting her arms around his neck from behind and pressing her cheek against his. 'Nothing you ever said could make me do that.'

He patted her hands. Then they both glanced at each other, hearing urgent knocking at the back door.

'Mr Christensen? Are you there? It's Myrtle Johnson.'

'Now what can she want at this hour?' Knud muttered, rolling his eyes. While he had always got on well with her husband, who had been an excellent stable foreman, he didn't have much time for Myrtle or Bill. He pushed back his chair and answered the door to find her standing there in an old pink chenille dressing gown and a pair of grubby, fake fur slippers. She seemed agitated and was wringing her hands.

'Oh, Mr Christensen, our Bill isn't here with you, is he? He never came home all night.'

'No.'

'It's so unlike him. Whatever he's doing, he always comes home. No matter how late it is.'

'I've not seen him since last night, Mrs Johnson. I'm sorry to say I had to terminate his employment yesterday.'

'I know. And he was so upset, poor lad. I thought he might be here, asking you to reconsider and give him his job back?'

'I'm afraid it's too late for that,' Knud said gently. 'It needs a special type of person to work with horses — a man like your husband. Unfortunately, Bill doesn't take after him.'

'It's that Jimmy Flynn, isn't it?' Myrtle's

eyes narrowed with malice. 'Ever since he got here, you put him first before everyone. I hope you know what you're doing. People can be too trusting sometimes.'

Knud raised his eyebrows, wondering what had provoked this stream of vitriol.

'And Jimmy was drunk last night. I saw him.' Myrtle nodded, folding her arms and glaring at Leila who had joined her father at the door. 'Miss Christensen tried to pull the wool over my eyes and say that he wasn't. But I know the effects of drink when I see it.'

'Mrs Johnson,' Knud said quickly before Leila could join in, adding fuel to the argument. 'As you can see, Bill isn't here. And as we have a busy morning ahead of us — '

'Oh, I'm going. Can't get rid of us fast enough, can you? Now you've got your new horse and your precious Jimmy Flynn.' So saying, she whirled and stamped across the yard to her own cottage.

'Whew!' Knud pulled a face. 'What a harridan. And I used to think she was such an agreeable woman.'

'Myrtle Johnson was never agreeable, Pa.' Leila smiled at the thought. 'Smarmy is the word you're looking for.'

* * *

Jimmy awoke to the sound of raised voices. The Johnsons were still arguing across the hall. Groaning, he pulled the pillow over his head and tried to get back to sleep but he could still hear the low rumble of Bob Johnson's voice and the staccato, hysterical tones of Myrtle. He heard her running downstairs and out of the house, not caring that the door slammed behind her, shaking the windows. Without her, there was peace for several minutes until she returned, screaming for her husband as she ran up the stairs.

'Get dressed, Bobby. We're going to look for him in the car.'

'Good God, woman,' he heard Bobby groan. 'Bill's nearly twenty. He's not a child any more. He's probably shacked up with some girl.'

'Over my dead body!' Myrtle screeched. 'All the more reason to run him to earth, then.'

Jimmy could have told her that Bill was well on the way to a drunken stupor last night and would have been no use to any girl, willing or otherwise. But, sensibly, he decided to stay out of sight until he was sure the Johnsons had left, Bobby grumbling about leaving before breakfast and Myrtle calling him a heartless, unfeeling father.

The house was quiet after they left, so quiet that Jimmy was tempted to go back to sleep but a glance at the clock showed him it was already after five. Normally, he would have been up an hour ago and on his way to the stables. But now, apart from his bruised nose, he was feeling so much better, he could see no reason to stay in bed. It had been such a long time since he'd experienced that blurring and dizziness, followed by double vision, he'd almost convinced himself it was a thing of the past. Now it had happened twice in a matter of weeks and he knew that it wasn't.

And Leila — Leila had been wonderful, getting him home in one piece and even seeing him safely to bed. He winced as he remembered calling her Dianne. What had possessed him to do that? Was it the proprietary way she had tried to take off his jeans, reminding him too much of Dianne's insistent, importunate hands? Of course she would assume Dianne was his girlfriend. He rested his head on his knees and groaned. There would be no point in trying to explain it now; anything he said could only make it worse.

He showered quickly, dressed and made himself a cup of instant coffee, wanting to take as little as possible from Myrtle's kitchen. In less than forty-eight hours now, the Johnsons would be gone and the cottage at Ocean's View would be entirely his own. He was looking forward to it. At the stables, he found Leila preparing several horses for a run on the beach, including Bluey.

'What are you doing here?' She regarded him with mock severity. 'After what happened last night, I was hoping you'd rest up for a while.'

'I'm fine, really. Forgotten about it already.'

'Are you sure?' She peered at him. 'You're lucky not to have a pair of black eyes.'

'Just drop it, Leila.' He lowered his eyes to avoid her penetrating gaze. 'Really — I'm OK.'

While some of the boys and Knud headed off to walk the horses on one side of the beach, Leila and Jimmy led Bluey and Party Animal to the other. At this hour of the morning there was a chill wind blowing off the sea, dawn had scarcely broken and there was no one about.

'And you?' he asked her at last. 'How are you feeling this morning? Not thinking of making it up with Brett Hanson?' The words were out before he could stop them. He waited for her to tell him to mind his own business but instead she answered him candidly without taking offence.

'No. I feel more like my own woman than I have for some time.'

'Good for you.'

'Ooh — speak of the devil,' she muttered half under her breath, catching sight of a male figure in shorts swaggering towards them from the dunes; none other than Brett Hanson, accompanied by Duster, his red kelpie. Whenever Brett was around the beach or his father's boats, Duster would never be far behind. A one-man dog of uncertain temper, he could be unpredictable and aggressive towards anyone else. 'We could pretend we haven't seen him and ride on with the horses. But I'll have to run into him sooner or later.' She sighed. 'Better find out what he wants.' And they stood beside the horses, waiting for Brett to catch up.

'Have you seen Bill?' He came straight to the point without any greeting. 'Some of us went for a dive to sober up after the party and he's taken off with one of my wet suits. I want it back.'

'Everyone seems to be looking for Bill this morning, including his mother,' Leila said. 'He didn't come home last night. I hope he's OK.'

'Bill's tough as old boots. He's always OK. I'll catch up with him later.'

Leila shrugged, turning her back on him

but Brett wasn't about to let her get off so easily. 'Your father didn't want to say where you were but I knew I'd find you at this end of the beach,' he said, giving Jimmy a hard stare. 'Can you give us a moment, Jim. I want to talk to Leila — alone.'

It was on the tip of Jim's tongue to say that Brett hadn't shown much care for privacy or discretion last night but realized that it wasn't his place to say so. In any case, Leila was already offering Party Animal's rein. Reluctantly, he accepted it, leading both horses away on the hard sand just above the shoreline.

'I know what you're going to say, Brett,' Leila jumped in before he could raise the usual argument. 'But I meant what I said last night. We're finished. I don't want to see you any more.'

'But what shall I tell my mother? You know how she loves you. She'll kill me when I have to tell her we're not getting married.'

'I could say you should have thought of that before.' Her lips twitched into a rueful smile. 'But never mind, I'm sure your Mum will be just as happy with Jenny — her father has much more money than mine.'

'Jenny? That spoiled brat? I'd sooner stitch my lips together with fishing line.'

Without meaning to, she laughed aloud.

'It's not funny, Leila. I don't know what's got into you lately.'

'*I* do. I've come to my senses. I've spent the last five years chasing after you, excusing you to my friends and even myself. But my heart no longer turns somersaults when I see you and I have to say it feels good.' So saying, she turned her back on him, expecting that to be the end of it.

He stepped forward and caught her arm, swinging her round to face him. 'Don't you turn your back on me, I'm not done with you, yet,' he said through clenched teeth. 'Where'd you get to last night? I looked for you in the early hours and you were nowhere to be found.'

'Really? Not till the early hours?'

'Then someone remembered they'd seen you leaving with Flynn.' He jerked his head towards Jimmy who was walking the horses further up the beach. 'Very chummy you looked, too.'

'I don't have to explain myself to anyone, Brett, least of all you.' Once more she tried to turn away but he seized her wrist, dragging her back again. 'Let go — you're hurting me.'

Duster, sensing the tension between them, barked fiercely, distracting Brett long enough to make him release his hold. Hearing the dog, Jimmy also turned and looked back to see what was happening. Hackles raised, Duster stood growling as Leila took a pace backwards, rubbing her bruised wrist.

'I should have left you a long time ago.' She spoke hesitantly, anger and emotion stealing her breath.

'Leila, please.' He seemed to realize at last that he'd lost her. 'If we're not together, can't we at least be friends?'

'I don't think so, Brett. I'm not even sure I like you any more.' She glanced at Duster who was still drawing back his lips to show her his teeth. 'And I certainly don't like your mean dog.'

Brett stood there for a moment, more stunned to hear her opinion of Duster than anything else. Then, whistling the dog to heel, he turned and walked slowly away from the beach without turning back.

Leila watched for a moment to make sure he was leaving before she jogged up the beach to catch up with Jimmy. Her heart was thumping — she hated scenes, and her wrist was still burning from Brett's rough treatment. Although her eyes were stinging with unshed tears, they were of relief rather than regret and she was still convinced she had done the right thing.

'Everything all right?' Jimmy glanced at her, noting the flushed face and the tears gathering in her eyes, as she reclaimed Party Animal.

She nodded, wide-eyed, unable to speak through the lump in her throat.

'We can take the horses back now, if you like,' he said, glancing at his watch. 'They might've had enough.'

'No,' she said, springing up to ride Party Animal bare backed. 'The tide won't be back for hours. We can go round the rocks and I'll show you the next cove — it's more sheltered than this one. We have picnics there in the summer.' So saying, she took off, leaving Jimmy to follow at his own pace.

Sensing she needed a few moments alone, Jimmy dawdled with Starshine Blue, taking his time before leading the horse round the rocks to the smaller bay beyond. It was small and picturesque with rocks tumbling down into the sea at either end. When he caught up with her, she had dismounted and Party Animal stood waiting beside her as she sat on a rock, hiding her face in her arms.

'Leila, don't hold back — it's OK to cry,' he said, putting an arm around her shoulders and sitting beside her. 'It can be hard breaking up with someone you've loved.'

'How d'you know so much?' She sniffed and sat up straight, recovering herself, although she made no attempt to move away.

‘Did it happen to you?’

‘In a way,’ he said. ‘How does the song go? *You were only teasin’ while I was falling in love*.’

‘Is that why you came to us, Jimmy? To get away from an unhappy love affair?’

‘Oh no.’ He smiled at the thought. ‘That was over a long time ago.’

‘Dianne?’

He nodded. ‘Uhuh. Clive Bannerman’s daughter no less.’

‘Clive’s daughter? Oh, dear.’ Leila raised quizzical eyebrows.

‘I see her reputation precedes her.’ He laughed shortly. ‘I wasn’t in favour for long. The stable foreman warned me off.’

‘And were you sorry to lose her?’

‘At the time. But I think Dianne and Brett come out of the same mould. I soon realized I’d had a lucky escape.’ She felt so right in the curve of his arm that he wanted to kiss away her tears and see her smile again but he knew it was too soon. This wasn’t the time. It was enough that she felt easy in his embrace. So he glanced away up the beach, squinting into the early morning sun as something caught his attention on the shoreline. It was a large figure, half in and half out of the water with seaweed shifting around it as the ripples came and went.

'What d'you make of that?' he said at last. 'Is it a seal?'

'No, that isn't a seal.' Leila shook her head. 'I'm afraid it looks more like a man. A man in a wet suit.'

Their eyes met as the same thought struck both of them. *Bill Johnson*.

'Stay here with the horses,' Jimmy said. 'I'll go take a look.'

He jogged the fifty yards or so and quickly recognized the prostrate figure as Bill Johnson, lying face down on the sand. Carefully, he turned the man over, hoping it wouldn't be too late to revive him and, without really knowing what he was doing, crossed his hands and pressed down on his breast-bone, commencing a resuscitation technique. He was hoping he wouldn't have to use mouth to mouth. To his relief, Billy coughed and sat up at once, bellowing hoarsely.

'Bloody hell, man! What you tryin' to do? I'm not drowned, I'm just fuckin' exhausted from fightin' the rip an' the current all night. I knew I'd get washed in here if I could hold on long enough.'

By now, Leila had come up with the horses. 'Are you all right, Bill?' She said.

'Fat lot you care. Your precious boyfriend and his mates just left me to drown out there.'

'Better get on home, Bill. Your Mum's worried about you.'

'Yeah. She'll be the only one who is.' The youth scrambled unsteadily to his feet, swerving away from Jimmy who reached out to help him.

'So what now, Bill?' Leila felt bound to ask. 'Will you go to Queensland with your parents?'

'You'd like that, wouldn't you?' He squinted at her through red-rimmed, bloodshot eyes. 'The Johnsons all tidied up an' gone. Nah. I'll probably stick around an' hang out with Brett for a while. Maybe get work on one of his father's boats. I've had it with stables and stinkin' horse shit.' He hawked and spat at their feet and, once more refusing a helping hand from either of them, he staggered away up the beach.

'A real charmer, isn't he?' Jimmy said.

'I'd change the locks on the cottage when you take over.' Leila was pensive, watching him. 'I wouldn't trust Bill to surrender his keys.'

'Why? I don't have anything worth stealing and anyway what can he do?'

'I'm not sure, Jim. But he's angry and resentful. I don't have a good feeling about him.'

* * *

Jimmy didn't know what to do. More than three weeks had gone by since Leila's break-up with Brett and she had remained true to herself, refusing to take the easy way out and go back. Several times, he had seen her blocking what must be Brett's phone calls, holding the button down until the phone stopped ringing. So far as Jimmy was concerned, he couldn't stop thinking about her. He was almost sure Leila might feel the same but still he didn't know how to make the first move. The last thing he wanted was to ruin things by making a mistake. After parting from Brett, she had made it clear that she was enjoying her freedom and being 'her own woman', as she called it. Probably, it was still too soon for her to take up with anyone else. Master of his own house now the Johnsons were gone, he had spent many a lonely evening brooding on this.

So it was a complete surprise when she turned up on his doorstep one Saturday night, made up to the nines with mascara lengthening her normally pale lashes and wearing an amazingly slinky tomato-red dress that clung to her figure in all the right places.

'Wha — ?' he started to say.

'Have a shower and get dressed in your best,' she said. 'We're going out.'

'We are?' He stared at her as if she'd

suggested a flight to the moon, quickly remembering to close his mouth.

'Yes. I've had enough of staying home and being a hermit and so have you. We're going out on the town to dine and then on to a nice little club where we can dance.' He was already opening his mouth to protest. 'And don't you dare tell me you can't dance.'

'Oh, I can dance all right,' he said. 'My sister taught me when I was twelve years old. I haven't forgiven her yet.' Still, he seemed hesitant, biting his lips.

'So what's wrong now?' She fixed him with a serious look. 'Are you saying I've read you wrong and you really don't like me? And any moment now you're going to 'fess up and tell me you're gay?'

'No, no!' he said, pulling her over the threshold and shutting the door quickly to prevent her getting away. 'Of course I like you — a lot. And I'm not gay.'

'I didn't think you were.' She smiled and tilted her head to smoulder at him through those amazingly painted lashes, making his heart lurch in his chest.

'Sit down and wait for me. Don't go anywhere,' he said. 'Give me five minutes.'

The five minutes stretched into more than ten and upstairs in the bathroom he had to take deep breaths to hold steady and avoid cutting himself while he was shaving. Finally, he reappeared resplendent in a brown leather patchwork jacket, a cream handmade shirt and a pair of expensive cords.

'Wow!' she said. 'Worth the wait.'

'I hope I don't have to wear a tie? I hate the things.'

'Not where we're going.' She came very close to him, breathing in his freshly applied cologne that suited him so well. 'What's that wonderful stuff you're wearing? Eau de Cat-nip?'

He laughed. 'Leila, what's got into you? I've never seen you like this.'

'I don't suppose you have.' She gave a throaty laugh that made shivers run down his spine. 'You've only seen the country girl in wellies, stamping around the stables. This is the deluxe version. I'll have you know I was a model for two years when I left school.'

'I can well believe it. Why did you quit?'

'I dunno. It got boring after a while.' She glanced at her watch. 'Lets go. I've booked us in for eight and it's nearly that now.'

Without the horsebox behind it, Jimmy's Toyota made short work of the island's roads. He kept glancing across to make sure it really was Leila sitting beside him and this sexy, glamorous creature wasn't a figment of his own fevered imagination. She directed him to a weatherboard, ranch-style bistro with a view looking out on the ocean. There was a wind blowing and the sea looked dark and menacing at this time of night. Inside, the bistro had a cosy 'cabin in the mountains' feel, with a welcoming open fire. The room was busy, people seated at most of the tables, eating or awaiting their dinner.

A sharp-faced blonde in a black skirt and crisp white blouse, smiled and waved as soon as she caught sight of Leila and came over to greet her with a kiss.

'Mwah! Leila, darling, we haven't seen you for ages.'

'No,' she said. 'I'm just getting out and about again after parting from Brett.'

The woman's eyes grew round. 'Nobody told me. You parted from . . . ?'

'Yes, Patsy,' Leila cut in, not wanting her friend to pursue that particular line of conversation. 'And I'd like you to meet our new stable foreman — Jimmy Flynn.' She turned to Jimmy. 'This is Patsy Fleet. She and her husband own the place.'

'Charmed, I'm sure' Patsy murmured. 'And friend of Leila's — of course.' Suddenly, she was all business, leading them to an alcove where they would eat in private, offering menus and pointing out the day's specials advertised on a blackboard. 'And tonight, we're doing a special reprise of the seventies — we have shrimp cocktail, beef Wellington and a baked Alaska for two.'

'I'm up for the shrimp cocktail and baked Alaska,' Jimmy confided when Patsy had left them to make their choice. 'Not sure about the beef Wellington.'

'Neither am I,' Leila smiled. 'With Patsy it's hard to know if she's teasing or not. One night she offered a difficult customer a calamari thickshake. You should've seen the guy's face.'

'I hope she doesn't make a habit of it.'

'Look. On the specials board they're advertising a whole flounder with salad and chips. We can have the baked Alaska afterwards.'

'Suits me.' Jimmy grinned.

The food arrived in record time and conversation lapsed as they did justice to it. Patsy's husband, Tony — also the chef — came out for a word with Leila.

'Good choice,' he said when he saw the demolished bones of the flounder on their plates. 'Our fish is all locally caught. Brought in fresh every day.'

There was indeed a spectacular baked Alaska to follow that came to the table flaming and so large they were hard pressed to finish it. Leila swallowed the last of the ice cream and wiped her lips, sitting back with a sigh. 'I couldn't eat another thing,' she said. 'Just as well we're going to dance it off.'

'Well now, I'm not sure if I — ' he started to say.

'Otherwise.' She set down her napkin and sat back, regarding him with a stern gaze. 'We can stay here and have coffee and you shall tell me your life history, starting with the day you were born.'

Immediately, he was on his feet. 'So, lead me to it. Let's dance.'

Although Leila tried to pay for the meal as she had invited him, Jimmy insisted on taking the bill and using his gold credit card to pay for it. Leila spotted it at once. And don't tell me *that* was a present from Clive Bannerman?'

'Well, it was,' he said. 'One of the perks. And while I was working there he used to pick up the tab. I have to service it myself now.'

After saying farewell to Patsy and praising the meal, Jimmy once more suggested they should go home. Disappointed, Leila stared at him with a wounded look in her eyes.

'And you don't have to look like that — it's not because I'm not having a great time,' he hastened to reassure her. 'But I'm worried about Bluey. He gets restless and skittish in a high wind.'

'This side of the island faces the open sea.

The wind won't be half as fierce on our side.'

'Even so, I'd feel happier if I could see he was OK.'

'You might as well be married to that horse,' Leila muttered.

'Now stop that,' he said. 'Don't ruin what has been one of the best evenings of my life. You know you don't have to be jealous of Bluey.'

'I'm not jealous of anyone.' She folded her arms and frowned. 'Least of all that blue-tailed nag.'

6

Back at Ocean's View, Jimmy found out Leila was right. Although there was a stiff breeze blowing off the sea, it was nothing like the howling gale that had almost blown them off their feet on the other side of the island. Still peeved with him for cutting the evening short, Leila muttered a perfunctory 'G'night', and turned aside to open the door of his car and get out. Jimmy reached across to prevent her.

'Leila, don't,' he said. 'Just because I need to check on Bluey, that doesn't mean I want the evening to end,' he whispered, giving her his keys to the cottage. 'Go and let yourself in and I'll be there in five to make coffee. I treated myself to one of those new espresso machines.'

'I don't usually drink coffee this late at night . . . ' she began, still miffed.

'There is nothing usual about tonight.' He smiled at her. 'Go on. Live dangerously for once.'

When he came back from the stables, ruefully admitting that everything was just fine, he found she had already started making the coffee, opened the old-fashioned stove to let the glow of the wood inside it warm the room and set cups and saucers out on the kitchen table. He took off his coat and hung it on the back of a chair before sitting down.

'The kitchen's the best room in this house,' she said, looking around. 'Your pine table and chairs are just perfect — much more comfortable than those horrible laminated things the Johnsons had. I think they had a cheek, asking you to pay for their awful old furniture. Even St Vinnie's wouldn't have wanted it.'

'I don't mind. At least I've got something to sit on while I look for something I like. So far this is the only room I've had time to make my own. The next thing I want is a decent bed.'

'A friend of mine has a furniture shop. I'm sure she'll give you a good deal.'

He smiled. 'Do all your friends have shops or bistros?'

'I was born and raised here.' She shrugged. 'It's a close-knit community.'

'I suppose it is. I've always lived in the middle of nowhere.'

'Yes, where did you grow up, Jimmy?' She seized the opportunity to find out more about him. 'And how did you form such a strong attachment to Bluey? Pa said you helped the mare birth him as a foal?'

'Nula didn't need much help.' He smiled at the memory. 'But I sensed he was going to be a champion even then.' Omitting to mention Kirkwood's Lodge or to say exactly where in New South Wales it might be, he told the story of the fire in the stables and the commitment he made to Starshine Blue that night.

'And all my father cared about was getting the insurance company to pay for it all,' he concluded, with some bitterness.

'Oh? Your father owns the ranch?' Leila was quick to pick up on this detail. 'I didn't know that before.'

'Among other things. It's only a small operation.' He shrugged, not quite telling a lie. Compared to the rest of James Kirkwood's business empire, the bloodstock ranch *was* relatively small.

'That's odd. Pa knows of most of the breeding stables. I've never heard him mention the name of Flynn.'

Jimmy shrugged again. 'Since it's the best part of a thousand miles from here that's not so surprising. But you must have heard of Errol?'

Leila's eyes grew round. 'You're related to Errol Flynn?'

'No. But it just goes to show how common the name is.'

She swatted him on the back of the head and waited for him to enlarge on it but he didn't. 'Honestly, Jimmy, getting information out of you is like pulling teeth. You're the most close-lipped person I know.'

'I've already said — there's nothing to tell. I'm a boring person, really. I went to Bannerman's from the bloodstock ranch and then I brought Bluey to Ocean's View. That's all there is.'

'I can't help feeling there's a lot you're not telling me. Your father and sister — surely, you keep in touch?'

'With my sister, Sally, yes — we talk about once a week and she's great. But my father and I can't see eye to eye about anything. We had another row when I went to his fiftieth birthday party in Sydney.'

'That's a shame. What about?'

'The usual. He thinks if he chips away at it long enough, he'll get what he wants. He said he had a desk ready for me and it was time I came to my senses and stopped playing nursemaid to a horse. I lost my temper and said I could think of nothing worse than living in the city, chained to an office desk. He called me an ungrateful whelp and we haven't spoken since.' He sighed. 'Sal hates it. She's always trying to get us to patch things up.'

'I'm sorry.'

'Don't be.' He laughed shortly. 'We're both doing what we want.'

Leila stood up and smoothed down her dress, glancing at her watch. 'The witching hour — I should go.' She glared at him with mock severity. 'And when I think we could have been dancing the night away — '

'We still can,' he said. 'I've got music here. D'you like Human Nature? Very danceable.'

'Who doesn't? But Jimmy, I don't know.' Suddenly, she was shy at the thought of dancing with him alone and started looking for an excuse to leave. Before she could find one, he was already galloping for the stairs, returning almost at once with a portable CD player. After moving the table and chairs back out of the way, he put on a disc, letting it play softly so that they would be the only people to hear it. He didn't want to disturb the horses or Knud who had promised to get up early to see to them, allowing him to take a rare day off.

Keeping her distance, Leila danced self-consciously at first until Jimmy caught her in his arms, surprising her by whirling her around, ballroom-style and then slowing to an easy rhythm and clasping her hand against his shoulder while he held her close, looking into her eyes which had widened with surprise. A tall girl, she almost matched his height, fitting easily into his embrace.

'You really *are* a good dancer,' she whispered, short of breath and suddenly not quite comfortable under the close scrutiny of those gold-flecked brown eyes.

'I told you. My sister made sure of it,' he said, trying to sound nonchalant and wondering if she would be able to feel the sudden thundering of his heart; the blood pounding in his veins. It felt so right to hold her; he could only hope she was feeling the same.

As the music slowed, he tilted her chin up and kissed her lightly, experimentally, ready to release her at once if she should push him away or stiffen in his embrace. Instead, with a small murmur of pleasure, she wound her arms around his neck and pulled him closer still, allowing him to deepen the kiss. It was a long kiss and they indulged in it for some time before breathlessness forced them to break apart, pink in the face and smiling. Gently, Leila ran a finger along his bottom lip.

'I just knew you'd be a good kisser,' she said.

'Leila, I wouldn't want you to think I was taking advantage . . . ' He knew he was speaking too fast but he couldn't stop himself. 'I really don't want you to think I — '

'Hey!' she said cuffing him on the shoulder. 'Lighten up. It was only a kiss. And I enjoyed it.' She gave a throaty giggle that set his blood pounding again. 'I really think I'd better go. Human Nature has much to answer for. I'll see you some time tomorrow, Jim. Enjoy your day off.'

'Leila. Oh, Leila, don't go yet.' He pulled her close again, murmuring into her hair and making her shiver with delight. All the same she slipped from his grasp and, smiling impishly, seconds later was at the door.

'Your kisses can be addictive, Jimmy Flynn. And you've given me quite enough to think about for one night.' So saying, she blew him another kiss from a safer distance.

After she left, he turned off the music and went to bed. Usually, sleep claimed him immediately but not tonight. He kept seeing Leila's smile and remembering how perfectly she had fitted into his embrace, as if they were made for each other. Could he believe it? Was the love real this time? He told himself not to be such a romantic fool — it was much too early to tell.

Leila, tossing in her own bed was troubled by similar thoughts. Only a matter of weeks ago, she had thought herself in love with Brett but all that had changed since Jimmy Flynn arrived in her life. She had sensed the possibilities the moment he took off his hat — the hat she had been laughing at — and met her gaze with those smiling, warm brown eyes. It felt as if someone had turned on a light in her world, changing it from ordinary black and white into glorious colour. And then, Brett had given her the perfect excuse to break it off. Certainly, she had been looking for one for some time but what if that hadn't happened? What if Brett had been faithful? Would she still have fallen in love with Jimmy Flynn? There! She had admitted it, if only to herself. And if she could fall in love so recklessly, so easily, did that mean she was just as fickle as Brett? And what would her father think of this sudden change of heart? And Jimmy himself? What would he make of her behaviour? Turning up on his doorstep, boldly asking him to go out? And wearing the red dress Brett had always hated because he said it made people notice her. She had never done anything like that before — even Knud had raised his eyebrows in amused surprise when he saw her, made up to the nines and ready to paint the town. She bit her lips, blushing at the memory.

But then she remembered the enthusiasm of his kisses and how completely at ease they had been in each other's arms. It had felt so comfortable, so right, it was almost familiar, like coming home. A good thing she'd left the cottage when she did or she would almost certainly have ended up in his bed. And on a first date, too! She cringed at the thought. That might be all right for some girls but not for Leila.

And, aside from the obvious chemistry, they had so much in common. Brett had never been able to understand her love for Party Animal and the other horses in their stable. Jimmy not only understood, he shared her devotion. But, for the time being, she felt she had done enough; she would leave it to him to make the next move.

She didn't have to wait very long. A few days later Jimmy caught up with her in the stables, gleefully brandishing a couple of tickets. 'We're going out on the town,' he informed her.

'Really?' She tried to suppress her lurch of excitement and keep her cool. It wouldn't do to look too eager. 'I thought you hated going anywhere near the city?'

'I'd brave even the city to see this man. Richard Marx is giving a concert. He's playing in Melbourne, but only for one night.'

'Richard Marx.' She pondered the name for a moment. 'Not the song writer? He's even written for Barbra Streisand, hasn't he? Oh, I love his music.'

'So does my sister. She was the one who introduced me to it — she and her friends were all potty about him in the eighties. I remember them all swooning over him and his shoulder-length mullet. Do I take it then that you'd like to go?'

'Try and keep me away.'

Although the concert was taking place at a small, old-fashioned theatre, they arrived in the city to find the venue packed, mainly with people in their mid-thirties. Most of the crowd looked liked university professors with their adult students. Fortunately, the supporting act was good, an acoustic guitarist with a wonderful voice who commenced promptly at eight and was quick to engage the audience and hold them in thrall.

But when Richard and his band took the stage after the interval, the crowd went wild. Several girls called out to him and one even said: 'You're beautiful!' making him pause for a moment to say, 'Am I single? I wasn't the last time I looked.' Then, to soften the blow, he offered them his piano player, who *was* single, embarrassing the poor man and making him cringe and hide behind his piano.

'The music you've paid for,' Richard quipped. 'The comedy is free.' Leila and

Jimmy smiled at each other, amused by his casual humour.

Deserting his usual favourite, the piano, for a series of amazing guitars, he played many of his old songs in a new way and soon the whole room was bopping, caught by the infectious rhythm of this modern rock and roll. The band was obviously hand-picked, the lead guitarist and other musicians all masters of their art. During the last hour, they stepped up the volume, making it impossible for the audience to remain seated and those in the stalls crowded towards the stage, dancing in the aisles. Unable to keep still, Leila and Jimmy were quick to join them.

All too soon it was nearly eleven, the evening was over and Richard was saying goodnight. 'We're not going to run away and hide in the dark,' he said. 'We don't do that any more. We'll just play two more songs.' And that's exactly what he did, giving the audience more than their money's worth.

Everyone left the theatre smiling and on the long drive back to the island, Jimmy played several of Richard's CDs, pointing out the difference between his rather romantic earlier work and the driving rock and roll they had witnessed that night.

Back at Ocean's View, Jimmy parked the

Prado outside the cottage and turned towards her. 'I hope you enjoyed it?' he said. 'Because I loved having you with me — I wouldn't have wanted to go by myself.'

'Of course I loved it. Richard Marx has a new and devoted fan.' She tried to give him a quick kiss on the cheek but he caught her face in his hands to kiss her lips.

Dizzy with longing for him, Leila felt herself melting inside and placed a hand on his chest to steady herself. 'First Human Nature and now this,' she said, trying to make a joke of it. 'Are you trying to seduce me with music, Jimmy Flynn?'

'I will use any mean trick that comes to hand,' he murmured in her ear. 'I want you and I mean to have you, Leila Christensen. No matter how long it takes.'

'Ooh, look at the time.' She glanced at her watch, unwilling to meet that penetrating gaze. His kiss and his final words had totally unsettled her. 'We'll get barely four hours before we have to be at the stables.'

'Four hours?' He gave her a lazy smile. 'I probably won't sleep a wink.'

* * *

A month or so later, Starshine Blue won another race, this time ridden to victory by

Simon Grant, Knud Christensen's regular rider. He had recovered from his previous injury that turned out to be only a sprain rather than a break to his arm. The race was run at Flemington in November on the last day of the Spring Racing Carnival. There had still been a large crowd to cheer him on, although Melbourne's racegoers were beginning to run out of steam after almost three weeks of continuous party-going, punting and fun.

Jimmy was parading the horse, prior to the presentation of the trophy to Knud Christensen and Simon Grant who couldn't stop grinning after winning such an important race. Jimmy kept a firm hold on Bluey, knowing how much he hated wearing the slippery, fringed silk blanket awarded the victor and advertising the sponsors of the race. These things always annoyed him, flapping around his legs.

As Simon went to weigh in, Knud felt someone clap him on the shoulder and turned to see it was Clive Bannerman.

'Congratulations!' Clive boomed as he crushed Knud's hand in his own. 'I knew you'd do well with my horse.'

They paused in the middle of shaking hands to provide a photo opportunity for the press photographers: the high profile trainer condescending to the man with the smaller stable. Leila also had to submit to his bone-crunching handshake and a whiskery kiss.

'I hope you're not going to tell me you've changed your mind and you want him back?' Knud teased him gently.

'Oh no, I think old Bluey has found his niche — for the moment at least. Jimmy, too.' Bannerman watched the handsome grey and his strapper as they moved in small circles, Jimmy pulling his baseball cap low and turning towards the horse as if shielding his face from view. 'Look at him, still shy on race day, even after all these years.' Shaking his head in amusement, Bannerman saw someone else he knew and moved on, hailing them in that loud voice that made everyone turn to look at him.

'I always think Clive was born in the wrong era,' Leila said, watching him stride across the turf. 'He should have been a cattle baron in America at the time of the Wild West.'

'Not he!' Knud gave a shout of laughter. 'Clive would be lost without his stretch limo, his champagne and his string of pretty PAs. You do know he can't even ride?'

'Really?' Leila said absent-mindedly, her mind running on other things. For instance, how to get round to telling her father that

Jimmy had asked her to marry him and that she wanted to accept.

Since the 'night of the red dress' and the concert following it, they had been inseparable. And, unless Knud was being deliberately obtuse, he must have realized it, too. All those evenings she had spent at the cottage, creeping silently back to the house after midnight.

The catalyst had been the arrival of Jimmy's new bed. She had gone with him to her friend's shop and, after looking at everything, he had chosen a king-sized divan.

'But are you sure it'll fit?' Val, the shopkeeper, was quick to offer advice. 'For a cottage, this queen-sized one might be a better choice — the base comes apart and the mattress is flexible.'

'No — it's the king-size or nothing.' Jimmy was firm. 'I'm tired of sleeping in beds that are far too short. I'll make the sitting-room into a bedroom, if need be. It's already set up for TV I don't have time to use a sitting room, anyway — when I'm home, I like to sit in the kitchen.'

'He knows his own mind.' Leila pulled a little face at Val. 'And he's nothing if not stubborn.'

'I can see that.'

'Hey!' Jimmy said. 'Stop talking about me as if I'm not here.'

'Be quiet,' Leila teased. 'Or I won't buy you a sheet set as a house-warming present.'

On the afternoon the bed was due for delivery, Leila helped him to move the Johnsons' dilapidated furniture into an empty shed. The only thing they kept was a large blackwood bookcase which had held Bobby Johnson's collection of books plus a couple of picturesque, old-fashioned basket chairs, still in good condition as the Johnsons had never bothered to use them.

The bed arrived as promised, together with the two sets of candy-striped cotton sheets that were a present from Leila. There was also a handmade patchwork quilt in autumn colours of russet, gold and green. Jimmy had seen it hanging on the wall in the shop and insisted on taking it, even though Val seemed reluctant to let it go.

'I have a friend who makes them,' she said slowly. 'That one's mine. I use it just to take orders, really. I can get one for you in whatever colours you'd like?'

'Well, I like those colours,' Jimmy insisted. 'And I'm sure she'll be happy to make you another. Name your price.'

Leila's eyes widened when she named it but Jimmy didn't even blink as he paid up again with his gold credit card. Val relented and threw in some pillows gratis and was all smiles when they left. In the space of an hour, she had made as much profit as she sometimes made in a week.

They put the bed together and made it up. It loomed large, even in the sitting room. As Val predicted, it would never have fitted into any of the bedrooms upstairs.

'Luxury!' Jimmy fell back against the pillows, enjoying the feel of crisp cotton under his head and patting the space beside him, inviting Leila to try it.

'Very nice,' she said cautiously, perching on the very edge of the bed.

'Oh, come here!' Jimmy pulled her into his arms, subduing her murmured protests with an extended kiss. All the same, she sat up as soon as he let her go and seemed ready for flight. 'What's wrong now? Don't tell me you're one of those girls who can't make love in the afternoon?'

'With the right person, I can make love any time.' She pulled her turtle-necked sweater hiding her lips and nose and setting his heart thumping again as she regarded him with those wide, grey-green eyes. 'I just don't want you to think I'm easy, that's all.'

'Easy? You are not easy at all. You'd have to be the most complicated, inquisitive person I know.'

'That's not what I meant and you know it.

Stop teasing me when I want to be serious.'

Slowly, he pulled her down into his arms again and commenced kissing her thoroughly. Although Leila's experience extended only to Brett whose love-making had always been selfish and impatient, she knew Jimmy intended these kisses to lead them a lot further than they had been before. More than once he had put his hands on her body but, so far, had never ventured inside her clothes.

This time, after kissing her until she was pink in the face and breathless, he whispered softly, close in her ear, asking her to take off her sweater.

'Only if you take off your shirt,' she whispered back. Holding his gaze, she sat up and did so, then unfastened the red, lacy bra she was wearing beneath, freeing her firm but ample breasts. He pulled the clip from her hair and let it tumble down over her shoulders, thinking that now she really did look like a Norse goddess.

'Oh Leila, you're so beautiful,' he murmured, drawing her once again into his arms.

'D'you think so?' She looked down at her breasts. 'Brett used to complain that they were too big.'

'The man's a philistine,' he murmured, giving himself up to the total appreciation of her body. She sighed as he moved his hands over her breasts, rousing her nipples until they were ready for his kisses. After a while, this wasn't enough and they tore off their remaining clothes to make love fiercely, unable to get enough of each other.

It was only as they were recovering themselves from the dizzying heights of passion that Leila realized they had been making love without any protection at all.

And that was two weeks ago now. Since then she had discovered she wasn't pregnant, unsure if she was relieved or disappointed, and they had been doubly careful ever since. She wouldn't have minded herself but she knew her father was old-fashioned enough to want to see her married before starting a family. She had always wanted children herself, although this had been another bone of contention with Brett, who didn't.

Two days ago Jimmy had asked her to marry him. They had been in the stables together, grooming Starshine Blue and when he asked her that loaded question, she had been unable to see his face. She stood up at once, trying to look at him over the horse's back.

'Did you just say what I thought you did?' She said, unable to keep the tremor out of her voice.

'It's quite simple.' He stood up, leaning

across the horse to smile at her. 'All you have to do is say 'no' or 'yes'.'

'Oh Jimmy, it isn't that simple at all. And we've been together such a short time — '

'Stop! That's your head speaking, isn't it? Not your heart. Listen to your heart, Leila, and I'm sure it'll tell you it wants the same as mine.'

'But . . .'

At this point the horse stamped, realizing that he was no longer the centre of their attention.

'It's all right, Blue, you don't have to be jealous.' Jimmy patted the horse's neck. 'You know you love her just as much as I do.'

'How do you know I'm not on the rebound from Brett?'

'To begin with, I'm quite sure you were.' Jimmy grinned. 'And I took shameless advantage of it.'

'Oh, be serious.' She stared at him. 'You can't ask a girl to marry you and then make a joke of it.'

'I was never more serious in my life. But if you really want me to wait for your answer, I will. Or do you want me to do the old-fashioned thing and ask Knud?'

She grinned at that. 'Well, I'm sure he'd appreciate it, if you did. But if we talk to Pa about this, I think we should do it together.'

At this point, her father's voice intruded on her thoughts. He had been speaking for some time and she hadn't heard a word he was saying.

'Leila, hello! Where are you?' He was snapping his fingers before her eyes. 'Good heavens, girl, you were lost in a daydream. I've been to the presentation, accepted the trophy and you're still standing here in the same place I left you before. It's almost time for Party Animal's race.'

The horses were already coming into the mounting yard, Party Animal led by Terry Bayliss, the new lad that Jimmy had hired to replace Bill. Young as he was, Terry was already a competent horseman who could ride track work for the stables, making him twice as useful as the sullen, overweight Bill. Simon Grant appeared on time, wearing the Christensens' colours of light and dark blue, ready to ride the gelding who seemed calm yet alert — a good way to be before a major race. All seemed to be well as he leaped nimbly into the saddle and rode the horse out past the massed display of colourful Flemington roses.

It was only a short race and in no time at all the horses were on their way. The pace was fast and Party Animal, who always liked to race ahead of the field, took up the leading position on the fence. He seemed to be increasing the distance easily until something went badly wrong. He veered sideways, losing his balance and blundering into the fence, compounding the disaster by trying to jump it. Fortunately, Simon prevented it, hanging on for dear life and helping the horse to regain his balance instead of crashing to the ground. Giving them a wide berth, the field quickly passed them as the Christensens watched in horror. Simon dismounted at once and led the horse in, hoping his injuries were no more than superficial as the vet on course arrived quickly to look him over and assess the damage.

'Simon, what happened?' Leila ran down to meet him, closely followed by Knud. 'He's never done anything like that before.'

'He was going fine until something scared him.' Simon frowned. 'Not sure what it was — a sound like balloons bursting. With all the yelling of the crowd, you wouldn't think it would bother him so much.'

'Balloons?' Leila stared at him. 'Party Animal has always been frightened of balloons and loud noises. That's how he got his name — it's a kind of joke. But not too many people know that, unless they've been working for us.'

'Hmm.' Simon looked thoughtful. 'Well, it

certainly cost us the race. You haven't made any enemies recently, have you? Someone you had to turn off?'

Leila glanced at her father, thinking at once of Bill Johnson. 'Oh no. It has to be just high spirits. Surely no one would do that on purpose?'

'Well.' Simon hesitated, still looking troubled. 'I know you haven't worried too much about security, living as far out as you do. But to be on the safe side, I'd hire someone to keep an eye on things for a while. Most people these days use in-house cameras to monitor the stables twenty-four hours a day.' He glanced at his watch, getting ready to leave them. 'Think about it, anyway.'

At that moment the vet joined them to give his verdict. 'Not good news, I'm afraid. He has cuts and lacerations above the flexor tendon. You'll have to rest him now and let your own vet keep an eye on him. I can't be certain when, if ever, he'll be ready to race again.'

'Well, it comes as no surprise to me,' Knud said that evening when Jimmy and Leila sat him down to tell him of their marriage plans. 'I have rarely seen two people better suited than you.'

'You don't think we're rushing things? That it's too soon?' Leila frowned, biting her lip.

'If you're sure and know your own minds, why waste time?' Knud said. 'With Party

Animal grounded, you can do with a different focus. And with the two of you here to take care of things, maybe I'll take that trip to Europe that I've been promising myself for some time. I've a fancy to look up my relatives, speak my own language for a while.'

'Pa!' Leila stared at him. 'I never realized you were homesick?'

'I'm not. I just want to look at different horizons for a while.'

* * *

As Jimmy was walking back to the cottage alone — they were all tired after the eventful day at the races — his mobile rang and he saw it was his sister, Sally.

'Well, hello stranger. You were supposed to ring me last week remember?' she said.

'I've been a little busy.' He smiled. 'Bluey won another race today.'

'You and that horse.' She sounded faintly exasperated. 'You think as much of that animal as you would a child.'

'Well yes, I suppose I do.'

'Jimmy, I just rang to say you won't be hearing from me for a while. I'm taking a trip to Rome and Amsterdam, mixing business with pleasure. Can't wait to look at the clothes in Rome.'

'Sounds great. And I have some news for you, too. I'm getting married.'

'Married? Oh my God, no! Not to that dreadful Bannerman girl?'

Jimmy laughed. 'Heavens, no. To Leila Christensen — my new boss's daughter. The girl I told you about.'

'Ye-es,' Sally said slowly, absorbing the news. 'I think you did. But it's all a bit sudden, isn't it? You can't have known her more than a couple of months. And then . . . ' She hesitated, unsure whether to go on.

'Then, what? What's the matter, Sally?'

'Jim, don't take this the wrong way but I hope she knows who you are?'

'Of course she does,' he said, deliberately misunderstanding her. 'Leila's my soulmate. And she's as crazy about horses as I am.'

'You haven't told her, have you?' Sally said flatly. 'Give me the wedding date Jim. I'll postpone my trip to Europe. I'm coming down.'

'Sally, no. Please don't do this.'

'Why not? I'm your only sister. I ought to be there.'

'Because — you're so obviously wealthy — too well-heeled and svelte with your Italian handbags and designer clothes.'

She laughed shortly. 'Well, I've heard of people leaving relatives off the guest list for not being up to scratch but this is the first time — '

'Sal, you know what I mean. I adore you but I can't have you here at our wedding.'

'Isn't she going to think that odd?'

'Not really. I've already told her I'm estranged from my father.'

'But not from me,' Sally said in a small voice. 'All right. You don't have to get in a state. I'll be disappointed to miss it but I'll abide by your wishes. And I won't say anything to Dad until after the event.'

'Thanks, Sal.' He heaved a sigh of relief.

'But before I go, Jim, let me give you a piece of advice. As your future wife, Leila needs to know what sort of family she's marrying into. And you need to tell her — soon.'

'What for? My life is my own. Dad washed his hands of me long ago.'

'Don't be too sure. You're his only son and will always be part of his world. Ultimately, he's not going to let you forget it.'

7

Leila's wedding was not turning out as she'd pictured it to be. Ever since she was a little girl, she had cherished a dream of floating down the aisle in a full-length white gown that sparkled with rhinestones, and carrying an enormous bouquet of lacy ferns and white roses. On either side, the pews would be overflowing with friends and well-wishers. Lacking close relatives herself, apart from her father, she had expected her bridegroom's family to make up the deficit, together with her many local friends. Aware of the rift between them, she didn't expect to see Jimmy's father but she had looked forward to meeting his sister, Sally. It was a shock to learn that she couldn't be there because she was overseas.

'Are you sure you don't want to postpone the wedding?' She peered into Jimmy's face, surprised to find that he wasn't more upset. 'I won't mind, if you'd really like her to be here?'

'Not a chance.' He pulled her close and gave her a quick kiss on the tip of her nose. 'It's Sally's own choice — she could have postponed her trip if she'd really wanted to.' He knew he was painting a cold picture of Sally and one that was quite undeserved but for now he needed to keep a distance between Leila and his family.

'It just seems awful that you'll have no one of your own at our wedding. Have you no uncles, aunts or cousins you'd like to invite?'

'Not really. Dad was an only child and my mother's relatives are long lost — they live somewhere remote in Ireland.'

'And you've never wanted to go there and meet them? You don't even have their address?'

He looked away, uncomfortable with these persistent queries. 'I suppose Dad has it somewhere but I've never seen any need to keep in touch.' Jimmy shrugged.

'Then there doesn't seem much point in having a big event.' Leila sighed, a little piqued by his casual response. 'My mother won't come — she scarcely remembers my birthday these days. We might as well say our vows in front of Pa and a couple of witnesses.'

'Would you really let us do that? Would you mind?' Clearly relieved, he accepted the offer before she could say it was only a gloomy joke. 'Why should we jump through hoops just to put on a show for everyone else?'

'No reason at all,' she said in a small voice, wilting a little in his embrace.

'Leila?' He picked up on her mood at once. 'Oh sweetheart, don't be sad. This is our day — it should be only for us. Instead of a conventional wedding with all the trimmings and stress, why don't we splurge on a fabulous honeymoon instead?'

'Well, really Jimmy, what I've always — '

'I know — you can choose. We'll go anywhere you want — just so long as we're only away for a week. Your father's marvellous, of course, and Terry's better than most but I've never left Bluey that long before.'

'You and that horse of yours,' Leila teased, echoing his sister's words.

'I'm serious, Leila. What shall it be? A cruise in the Whitsundays? A penthouse apartment on the Sunshine Coast? An escape to nature in a tropical rainforest?'

'Stop!' She laughed weakly. 'Nobody's ever offered me so many luxuries all at once.'

'Just say the word and it's yours.'

'With money no object? Who *are* you, Jimmy Flynn?'

He smiled and shrugged again. 'Just someone who loves you very much.'

'I can't decide between the tropical rainforest and the reef. I've always wanted to see a rainforest — those great tall trees and all the exotic birds and animals, the tropical butterflies.'

'Then the rainforest it shall be. In fact, if we go to Port Douglas, we can have the best of both worlds, the rainforest and the reef.'

'You've been there before?'

'My father took me there once — when I was a lot younger, of course. We were supposed to go on a fishing trip but he got caught up with business and sent me off in the care of the skipper instead.'

Leila looked at him, seeing him in her mind's eye as a lonely boy whose father never made time for him.

'You don't have to look like that.' He grinned at her woeful expression. 'I had a better time than I would have with Dad. The skipper let me drink beer and reel in my own fish.'

'Your father sounds like a bit of a monster.'

'No. He's just a workaholic who doesn't know how to stop.'

'I still think it's a pity you don't get on. It's not too late to ask him to come to the wedding.'

'Believe me, Leila, it's way too late for me to mend fences with him. In the case of my father, I promise you, it's best to let sleeping dogs lie.'

And now the day was here, she couldn't help but draw comparisons between the wedding she had dreamed about for so long and this plain reality. Even the sky remained overcast as if in disapproval of the frugal arrangements that had been made. Instead of the civil ceremony suggested by Jimmy, Knud had insisted the wedding take place in the local Anglican church although neither he nor his daughter were regular churchgoers. The elderly vicar, pressed into service for the occasion, seemed all too mindful of that fact.

Surprisingly, she did have a beautiful dress. Among the clothes her mother had left behind, perfectly preserved in tissue paper in an old trunk, was a classic oyster satin cocktail dress from the fifties, with a slender skirt and a strapless bodice covered in pale mother-of-pearl sequins, with a small figure-hugging short jacket to match. The label said it had been handmade in France and there was even a pair of matching high-heeled shoes that almost fitted, apart from pinching her toes. She was sure it had never belonged to her mother. Until Inga had gone to South America, she had favoured a gypsy style of embroidered, peasant blouses worn with colourful, swirling skirts. She embraced style and fashion only when she acquired a husband who could afford to indulge her new taste for expensive clothes. Given the age of the dress, it had probably belonged to her grandmother. Inga must have kept it because it was just too lovely to give away. And when she tried it on, Leila found out it must have been worn with a corset because until she gave in and bought herself a modern equivalent, the zip wouldn't fasten with ease. Now, with her figure controlled and her head held high by the stand-up collar, she knew she looked every inch Jimmy's Nordic princess.

Although it was early summer, the church remained cool, the more so because it was empty apart from Tony and Patsy Fleet, roped in as witnesses and Jimmy himself, standing in front of the vicar alone. The minister, dressed in robes so white he looked like a washing powder advertisement, peered over his spectacles at the approaching bride. No welcoming smile for her. The lack of guests and festive decorations for the church had led him to believe this must be a 'shotgun' wedding, cobbled together in haste.

Patsy Fleet, never the most tactful of Leila's friends, had come right out and said the same thing when Leila called at the bistro to ask the Fleets to stand up as their witnesses.

'Only too happy to oblige.' Patsy regarded her, head on one side. 'But you always told me you wanted a real white wedding. Why aren't you having your big day out?' Her eyes widened as a thought struck her. 'Leila! Oh God, you're not pregnant, are you? Or is it

Jimmy? Has he been married before?'

'Come on, Patsy, he's only twenty-five — of course not.'

'Oh, I've known people marry at nineteen and have it all end in tears by the time they're twenty.'

'Well, aren't you the cheerful one?' Leila smiled ruefully, shaking her head. 'But no. I'm not pregnant and Jimmy hasn't been married before.'

'Hm.' Patsy regarded her in turn. 'Well, I can't put my finger on it but there's something about that young man. He seems almost wary — never speaks without thinking it over first. I hope you get to the bottom of whatever the mystery is.'

'Patsy, believe me. There is no mystery. Jimmy only comes across as wary because he's shy.' She felt a flash of irritation. 'And if you and Tony don't want to be our witnesses, we can always ask someone else.'

'Oh, come off your high horse.' Patsy gave her a quick hug. 'I say these things only because I love you. Of course we'll be there.'

* * *

Although the church was all but empty, Leila felt a flutter of nerves as her father smiled down at her and tucked her hand in his arm, leading her towards her groom. Even today, Jimmy was dressed in his casual clothes; he probably didn't even possess a suit. But when she reached his side, he turned and looked at her with such emotion and love in his eyes that she drew a shuddering breath and smiled radiantly back. All her doubts faded; she knew it was going to be all right.

The vicar gave them the briefest of ceremonies with no homily and no hymns. Barely ten minutes later they were standing outside the church as he turned away, locking up behind them.

'Disagreeable old thing,' Patsy muttered, not quite out of his hearing. 'And he calls himself a Christian, I suppose.'

'Patsy! He'll hear you.' Leila suppressed a giggle.

'Come on, you two — and you, Knud . . .' Patsy included the bride's father in her invitations. 'We're not letting you go back to Ocean's View and the horses with no celebration at all. I've arranged a small private supper for us before we open up. It's our wedding present to you both.'

'Oh, Patsy, you're too good.' Leila hugged her, excited.

'Well, someone other than James here should have the chance to admire you in that wonderful dress.'

The bistro was in darkness when they arrived which Leila thought odd — usually the signs would be lit up and the kitchens would already be in action at least an hour or so before normal opening time. Patsy opened the door and ushered them towards the back room kept for private parties. As they entered the room, blinking in the glare of so many lights switched on at once, they were greeted with a shower of confetti and rice.

'Surprise!' The cry went up as Patsy led a round of applause for the bride and groom. Leila stared around, smiling as she recognized the people crowding forward to kiss her or shake her hand. Most of their friends were here, including some of the stable boys. Only Jimmy, eyeing the cub reporter from the local newspaper and his cameraman, seemed less than delighted.

'Who's looking after the horses?' he whispered to Knud. 'After that incident at the races . . . '

'Stop worrying about them, they'll be fine,' Knud whispered back. 'Young Terry's very responsible and Ben will be there to help him.'

'A nice close-up of the bride and groom.' The reporter urged his cameraman towards them. 'Racing personalities and you getting hitched to the boss's daughter . . . ' he murmured to Jimmy, giving him a sly wink. 'Might even make the nationals.'

'Now look here!' Jimmy was icy calm but the tremor in his voice betrayed his suppressed feelings. 'This is exactly why we didn't want a fuss. We are having a private celebration and we'd be grateful if you would leave us alone to enjoy it — now!'

'All right, all right. Sorry, I'm sure.' The cub reporter rolled his eyes. 'Most people can't wait to see their faces in print.' He turned to his cameraman. 'Lets get out of here, Ron. See what else we can find.'

'Oh, dear.' Patsy watched them leave. 'Did you have to be so tough on him, Jimmy? I know he's only a kid but the local paper wields quite a lot of power around here.'

After this, the party progressed without incident although it broke up early. Knud would be up with the horses as usual and the newly-weds were to catch a plane to Cairns in the early hours of the morning. With a stop in Sydney, it would take most of the day to reach their destination.

In the early hours, Knud was up making porridge for all of them and it should have been a relaxing time except that Jimmy seized the opportunity to bombard Leila's father with the long list of instructions he thought he needed to take proper care of Bluey.

'Good heavens, boy!' At last Knud's patience was wearing thin. 'I've looked after horses for over thirty years and never lost an animal for the lack of care. Go on your honeymoon, the pair of you. Enjoy yourselves and don't be ringing me up every five minutes to make sure that great brute is OK.'

* * *

Several hours later, Leila peered out of the window fascinated by the aerial view of Sydney as the plane descended.

'Look!' she said. 'I can see the Opera House and there it is — there's the rusty coathanger!'

'D'you mind?' Jimmy frowned with pretended severity. 'As a Sydneysider, I take exception to that.'

'*Are* you a Sydneysider, Jimmy? You never said so before.'

'Not really. But New South Wales is my home state and I'm proud of it.'

On this occasion, they didn't see much more of Sydney than the inside of the airport and they were soon on their way again. After several more hours in the air and having watched several in-flight movies, during which Leila had dozed with her head on her new husband's shoulder, the pilot announced that shortly they would be descending towards Cairns.

To Leila the air seemed stifling as they got off the plane. She had forgotten that at this time of year — almost Christmas — the tropics would be hot and humid. She was grateful to reach the air conditioned comfort of the airport terminal.

While she waited for their luggage, Jimmy went to collect the car he had hired and when they rejoined each other, she was pleased to see it was a serviceable station wagon. He piled in their luggage that now appeared to include two rolled up sleeping bags she didn't remember seeing before.

'What do we need those for?' she asked.

'Well, I thought we'd take pot luck with accommodation. If we can't find anywhere we like, we can always camp and sleep in the car.'

Leila's smile faded. Suddenly, it seemed they were about to have the first disagreement of their married life.

'Great!' she said. 'I didn't give up my dream of a full-blown white wedding just to go on a camping holiday. Haven't you noticed how hot and humid it is up here? We shall be stifled if we try to sleep in that car.'

He looked at her properly then, seeing she really was getting annoyed. This was something he hadn't encountered before. 'Well, no.

No, of course not. We'll stay wherever you like.'

'Jimmy, hello! It's nearly Christmas, the resorts will be packed and you're telling me you haven't even booked us a room?'

'Look. There are hotels in Cairns. Hotels and resorts all the way up to Port Douglas and beyond — and you did say you wanted to see the rainforest.'

'Yes but in a civilized way like any other tourist. I don't want to see it at such close quarters that I'm sharing the night with giant mosquitoes and anything else that happens to be around.'

'Calm down. I'm sure we'll be able to find the perfect place.'

'I wish I could share your optimism. Let's put it to the test, shall we?' So saying, she hopped into the passenger's seat in the car and sat glaring out of the window, arms folded and lips pursed.

Jimmy, having never seen this side of Leila before, eased himself into the driver's seat and took off slowly and smoothly, as if afraid any new jolt of the car might provoke a new tirade. He drove away from the airport and followed the signs directing them north to the winding coast road which would take them to Port Douglas.

'It's just nerves,' he muttered to himself.

'Honeymoon jitters, that's all.'

She turned towards him, still fierce. 'What did you say?'

'Me? Nothing.' He shrugged.

Unfortunately, as Leila predicted, most of the smaller, more picturesque places were indeed fully booked and she refused to stay in any of the larger ones, saying it would be the same as putting up in any high-rise hotel in Melbourne. They were tired and hungry by the time they reached Port Douglas and Jimmy insisted they should stop and have dinner before resuming their search. He was hoping a full stomach might improve Leila's mood.

He chose a small, friendly bistro on the main street of the town and ordered a simple meal of fish and chips, surprising the proprietor by asking for a bottle of vintage Chandon to go with it.

'So what's the occasion?' The man smiled, pouring the sparkling liquid into a glass for Jimmy to taste before filling both their flutes.

'We got married yesterday — ' Jimmy started to explain.

'And as yet we have nowhere to stay.' Leila finished the sentence for him, her eyes still wide with reproach.

'Really?' the man said. 'Well, I just might be able to help you there. My sister and brother-in-law just finished building a new place on the outskirts of the town. It's barely open for business but, if you like, I'll ring them to see?'

'It isn't a big hotel, is it?' Leila said. 'Can't stand places with lifts and twenty floors.'

'Oh, it isn't like that, not at all.' The man seemed shocked at the idea. 'No. I'd say it's much more like a family motel. Only half a dozen suites, all private and with their own outside areas. They'll provide tea and coffee but otherwise it's self-catering. Oh, and if it's finished, there's a lovely barbecue area alongside a big pool, shaped like a clover leaf, surrounded by palms and bird's nest ferns.'

'But it sounds ideal — just what we're looking for.' Leila smiled for the first time in several hours. 'I do hope they're ready for visitors.'

'I'll call them and see.' The café proprietor smiled back.

John and Julie Soames, who owned Corner of Paradise were quite young but very enthusiastic, explaining that prior to getting married and setting themselves up in the hotel business, they had both been professional tennis players. Photos of both of them in action at Wimbledon and Melbourne Park decorated the foyer. Injury had forced John off the circuit and Julie opted to retire at the same time. The last lick of paint had been added the day before, the pool had only to be filled and the water tested for them to be ready and open for business. They asked Leila and Jim to sign the visitors' book as their very first guests and offered them the deluxe honeymoon suite, overlooking the pool which Julie promised would be ready for their use the next day.

When they were left alone, Leila finally made her peace with Jimmy. 'I'm so sorry,' she said. 'I don't know what came over me. I nearly ruined our day.'

'But you didn't.' Jimmy enfolded her in his embrace. 'And look — we have more than just a suite to ourselves, we have a whole motel.'

'I should've known we'd find somewhere. I just didn't want to camp — '

'Or end up in a high-rise hotel.' He finished the sentence for her. 'Well, we are properly married now — we very nearly had our first fight.'

As the recess was large enough, they showered together, using the lavender-scented toiletries provided by the motel. They soaped one another in business-like fashion at first until their hands slowed into a languid rhythm as they washed the more sensitive areas of each other's bodies. Closing her eyes,

Leila sighed and leaned in towards him, letting him feel the tautness of her breasts against his chest, demonstrating without words her readiness to make love. He kissed her deeply, making her wait a little longer, letting the water sluice down her hair and back before lifting her into his embrace.

'Oh now, please,' she murmured into his mouth as she guided him towards her throbbing need. Somehow, that 'almost quarrel' had increased their sexual arousal and she wanted to draw him in and smother him, assuring him of her love. It was over too quickly because they were both excited, both by the unfamiliarity of their surroundings and because this was the first time they had made love anywhere but in Jimmy's king-size bed.

Afterwards, having dried themselves in luxurious white bath sheets, they lay on the enormous, heart-shaped bed and gazed into each other's eyes.

'We *are* going to be happy, aren't we, Jimmy?' she murmured.

He ran a finger down her nose and kissed her lightly on the lips. 'Well, Mrs Flynn, I think it's a little late for second thoughts.'

'Oh, I didn't mean I'm not happy right now — I am. I'm just hoping it's not too wonderful to last.'

'Leila, I can't promise the world will never

change,' he said, catching the seriousness of her mood. 'Because change is inevitable, it's happening every day. But I can promise you will always have my love — from the moment I saw you, I knew there would never be anyone else, not for me.'

'Oh, Jimmy that's so — so . . . ' Almost choked by emotion, she pushed a stray lock of dark hair out of his eyes. 'No one could ask for anything more than that.'

'Then what is it? What's making you sad?'

'I'm not sad. I was just remembering something Patsy said.'

'Oh? What was that?'

'She called you a man of mystery.'

Jimmy crowed with laughter, perhaps more than such a simple remark deserved. 'Look, I'm sure Patsy's a lovely girl but she doesn't get out enough — always searching for mysteries where there are none. Really, she should get busy and write it all down — she'll be the new Agatha Christie.'

'You don't have to get angry. I'm only telling you what she said.'

Suddenly, he sat up in bed and glanced at his watch, his mind clearly running on something else. 'It's still only eleven o'clock.' He reached for his mobile. 'I might give Knud a quick ring, make sure Bluey's all right.'

'No!' Just as quickly she sat up and snatched it out of his hand. 'Pa will have been asleep for at least an hour now. We can call him tomorrow, if you must.'

'I just want him to know where we're staying, in case anything goes wrong. You know he hates ringing mobiles.'

'Jimmy, in the space of a week, nothing is going to go wrong. And if it does, Pa will deal with it. He's a good horseman and with far more experience than both of us.'

'I know — it's just . . . '

'We are here on our honeymoon. This is not a rehearsal — it's real. By extraordinary good fortune, we've found exactly the right place to stay. Let us make a pact now to enjoy it completely. I promise not to think about Patsy or anyone, not even Pa. And you're not to think of Bluey — at least not until we can see Melbourne again from the plane.'

'Not even one little phone call in the morning?'

'Not even.' She held the phone away from his grasping fingers. 'You have to promise or I'll throw your phone in the pool.'

'The pool's empty,' he reminded her.

'Still wouldn't do it any good.'

'All right, I promise,' he said, leaning over her with a pirate's grin and making her squeal in mock fright. Then he tickled her, recovering his phone and making her shriek. 'But I shall need entertaining twenty-four hours a day to keep my mind off it all.'

In the morning, she got up and looked in the mirror, smiling at her wild hair and lips still swollen and tender from so many kisses. Her husband lay spreadeagled on the bed, fast asleep and with a satisfied smile on his face, the sheets rumpled around him. Seeing that it was past nine o'clock, she was about to wake him when there was a soft tap at the door. She put on a robe and hurried to answer it.

Julie was standing there with a tray of steaming coffee, fresh croissants and strawberry jam. 'We don't usually cater but I know you didn't have time to shop last night so I thought you could do with this,' she whispered with an impish grin, taking in Leila's flushed face and wild hair. 'Hope I'm not interrupting anything?'

'No, and that smells wonderful, thank you,' Leila whispered back. 'Just what we need.'

'The boys are filling the pool right now. Should be ready in an hour or so.'

'Thanks,' Leila whispered again.

'You don't have to whisper, I'm awake,' Jimmy said behind her, yawning and stretching. 'And rr-ravenous!'

After breakfast, they were surprised to find

themselves ready to make love again. While neither could be said to be connoisseurs in the art of making love, they were both athletic enough to want to experiment with different positions. It seemed they couldn't get enough of each other and the more they made love, the more they wanted to start all over again.

Leila surfaced at last, shocked to see it was almost midday. 'Where did the morning go?' She stared at herself in the mirror, seeing her hair looked wilder than ever. 'Do you have enough energy left to go for a swim?'

He lay back on the bed, laughing weakly. 'So long as you pull me out, if I look like falling asleep and drowning.'

'Come on, they've filled the pool for us. We should at least show willing and use it.' He was still sprawled on the bed when she came back for him after taking a quick shower and putting on her modest, one-piece black swimming costume.

'How very nun-like,' he teased. 'Don't you have a bikini?'

'As a teenager, I wasn't allowed. My Pa's more old-fashioned than you think. Anyway, I can swim faster in this.'

When they emerged from their suite, they found John and Julie had already been swimming and were lying on two of the loungers under the palm trees.

'Afternoon, honeymooners,' Julie teased, smiling at them. 'The water's fine.'

Preparing to dive in, Jimmy issued a challenge to Leila. 'Race you to the end of the pool and back again. Right?'

And without waiting for her reply, he took off in an efficient crawl quickly reaching the other side of the pool. Arriving there, slightly breathless, he was surprised to find Leila was there right beside him. She turned more efficiently than he did and was soon leaving him at least four yards behind. Suddenly, she appeared to falter, losing her even rhythm and he overtook her easily to beat her by at least ten seconds. He climbed out on the deck and reached down to help her out of the water.

'Leila, are you OK?' He pulled her up into his embrace. 'What happened? You're a much better swimmer than I am. You were yards ahead and should've beaten me easily. Why didn't you?'

'It's silly really.' She looked away, unwilling to meet his gaze. 'I'd rather not say.'

'No, tell me.'

'It's because of Brett,' she said. 'He was always challenging me to swimming contests and then he'd go into a sulk for days if I won.'

'Leila, I'm not Brett and I hope I'm absolutely nothing like him. Now I want you to swim again and this time you don't hold back. If you can beat me, I want you to do so and be proud of it.'

This time she beat him easily, John and Julie applauding her win, and this time it was her turn to reach in and haul him out of the water.

'And how does that feel?' he asked her.

'Good.' She kissed him, glowing and breathless. 'Really good.'

8

Their week in Port Douglas was almost over. For Leila, the days had flown, merging one into another as a succession of new experiences and delights. And, although there were times when Jimmy cast a wistful eye on his mobile, he managed to get through the week without pestering Knud.

Apart from a few memorable trips to see the sights, their days had been spent lazing alongside the pool at Corner of Paradise and their nights in each other's arms. They had lunched in a tree house restaurant overlooking the Mossman River with the rainforest beyond. And when they went for a walk beside the stream after lunch, Leila pointed out bright, tropical flowers and huge, jewel-coloured butterflies sunning themselves on the rocks. Some of the denizens of the forest were less enchanting though; giant mosquitoes and March flies hunting them for their blood.

Perhaps the highlight of the week was their cruise aboard a traditional Chinese junk, taking them on a leisurely journey to the inner reef. Being small, the vessel carried only a limited number of tourists and the laid-back, lazy atmosphere was totally in keeping with their mood. When they arrived at a quiet spot named the Blue Lagoon, where they were told they could swim in safety, they borrowed snorkels and flippers so they could examine the reef at close quarters. The water was turquoise blue and clear enough for them to see right down to the sand at the bottom. There they watched spiny sea urchins, inching slowly along the sand amid the treacherous spikes of living coral. They saw brightly coloured tropical fish darting among soft corals that waved like undersea plants and enormous, barnacle encrusted clams, their bright blue lips wide open until they were disturbed when they closed them with a snap and a puff of sand. The living colours of the reef and the fish were so brilliant and intense, they seemed almost unreal. And when the honeymooners finally tired of snorkelling, they sat on the beach with their toes in the water, gazing at the other tourist vessels on the horizon and running their fingers through sands that whispered and shimmered as if they were made of ground pearls. And when their little party was called back to the junk to make the homeward journey, nobody wanted to leave.

On the way back, the skipper announced

they were making good time and there was enough wind for him to cut the engines and rely totally upon sail. As he did so, the whole rhythm of the vessel changed, seeming much more in tune with the ocean. The silence and gentle slap of the waves was soothing after the relentless throb of the engines and smell of diesel fuel that always accompanied it.

Pleasantly tired after spending so long gazing at the wonders of the reef, Leila and Jimmy sat side by side on the deck, their arms around each other, watching the sun go down. It was still almost too bright to look at; a huge golden orb which appeared to melt into the horizon, staining the sea with reflected molten gold.

'Penny for them,' Jimmy breathed into her ear, hugging her close.

She turned towards him, daring a small kiss and hoping not to be teased for it. Somehow, everyone on board had found out they were honeymooners. 'I was thinking I've never been so happy in the whole of my life and I wish we didn't have to go home at all — that time would stand still and we could sail forever into the sunset together.'

'Ah yes, that's all very well but what about — '

She turned swiftly to look at him. 'And don't you dare mention Starshine Blue.'

'Why not? You just did.'

'Jimmy, be patient. You'll see him in less than two days. He probably hasn't even noticed you're gone.' At soon as the words were out, she regretted them, seeing the shadow of hurt in his eyes. 'I'm sorry! That sounded so bitchy — I didn't mean.'

'It's all right. I can't expect you to understand how I feel about Bluey.' He sighed. 'He's never really been mine although there's a bond between us stronger than most human ties. Clive Bannerman took him when he was two years old and I spent the next six years living in fear that he'd lose interest in him, have him gelded or just sell him off like he sold so many others. I worked tirelessly to keep him on top of his form and ready to win.'

'And he's a credit to you, Jimmy. He still is.'

'I know. But I was never more relieved than when Clive sold him to Knud. Suddenly, the pressure was off. I'd heard of your father by reputation and when I met him, I knew the horse would be treated well.'

'Did you never think of buying him back for yourself?'

'Well, I thought of it, sure. But even if I'd had the money, where would I keep him? Bluey's a champion, used to four-star accommodation And, as you pointed out to me once before, eventually he'll have to join a breeding stables and go to stud.'

'Your father wouldn't take him back?'

'My father never takes anything back.' Jimmy's expression clouded. 'With him, it's always on with the new.'

'You could always let Bluey retire and stay home with us. Even if Party Animal never races again, I won't let him go.'

'Leila! You'll end up with a stable full of old crocks.'

'I don't care. Keeping thoroughbreds isn't all about winning, you know.' She smiled briefly, struck by a different thought. 'You didn't think Pa made his money only from racing, did you?'

'I suppose so. Why? What else does he do?'

'We're not wealthy by any means — don't think you've married an heiress. But there's a small family business in Copenhagen. I think Pa holds half the shares already but there's an old aunt who has to be almost ninety and when she goes, he'll have even more. I think that's why he wants to go on this trip to Europe — to see her before she dies.'

Jimmy tensed, wondering if this was indeed the right moment to follow his sister's advice and explain that he was James Kirkwood junior and the heir to millions. He drew a deep breath, about to speak when Leila's next remark decided him against it.

'We don't make a big deal about it. Pa's always preferred the simple life. People treat you differently if they think you have money.'

'Yes,' he said thoughtfully, realizing that he had become so used to himself in the persona of Jimmy Flynn, it was only when he talked to Sally that he remembered where he came from. 'Yes, I suppose they do.'

* * *

When they arrived home, Melbourne was in the grip of a heatwave, the climate not so different from the one they had left some two thousand miles away. Their euphoric mood lasted only until they arrived at Ocean's View where they found Knud seated at the kitchen table with a substantial bandage wrapped around his head.

'Pa, whatever's happened?' Leila rushed to put her arms around him. 'You've had an accident?'

'You could say that. And be careful.' He winced in her embrace. 'Don't crush me, girl. You'll set my head throbbing again.'

'How did it happen? And why didn't you call us?'

'Ah now, what could you do? It was only

two days ago. Why should I spoil your honeymoon just because some idiot gave me a bump on the head.'

'Someone *did* this to you?' Jimmy was suddenly stern. 'Who?'

'I didn't see. Terry and the boys had gone off to see a film and I was just checking that all was well with the horses before going to bed. I must've surprised the intruder and he clouted me on the back of the head with a shovel. I went down like a ton of bricks. Didn't remember anything until Terry arrived back an hour or so later and insisted on taking me to the hospital. It must've looked a lot worse than it was — scalp wounds bleed a lot.' He pulled a face. 'I had six stitches and a tetanus injection. I'm not sure which was worse.'

'And — and the horses?' Jimmy seemed half afraid to ask.

'Fine, thank God. I must've disturbed the fellow before he could do any harm; he must've run off scared — probably didn't mean to hit me so hard. Even so, I called the vet out to check up on all of them and he took blood samples to be quite sure. So far nothing's come of it. Everything seems to be OK.'

Jimmy visibly relaxed although he was still troubled. 'But you were assaulted. Didn't you report it to the police?'

'What for? I didn't see who it was. Most likely just kids up to mischief in the school holidays.'

'I don't think so, Pa.' Like Jimmy, Leila was in no mood to make light of it. 'It could have been Bill Johnson. I think he was the one who frightened Party Animal at the races, too.'

'Now Leila, you've no proof of that. It could have been anyone. And I've taken my own precautions, in any case. We now have an in-house security system — look!' He indicated a closed circuit monitor installed on a shelf high up in the kitchen. 'Now we can see what's happening in any part of the stables, day or night. And for good measure, I've engaged an armed security guard to keep an eye on things overnight. If the intruder wants to come back, he'll find more than he bargained for.' He started showing Jimmy how to use the security system and they smiled at each other, watching Bluey enjoying a hose-down from Terry after his swim.

Leila glanced at her watch. 'I'll just pop out and get some supplies. Won't be long.'

The two men showed no sign of hearing this and didn't even look up, so engrossed were they in their new toy. She knew Jimmy would now spend some time catching up with Starshine Blue and there was a call she wanted to make. If she were to catch Brett Hanson's tourist boat when it came in just after five, she would have to hurry. So, without even asking permission, she took the Prado.

She parked directly opposite the pier so as to see the vessel arrive and didn't have to wait long. As soon as the boat was secure, sun-scorched visitors clambered ashore, some carrying plastic bags weighed down with their booty, others still a little green under the sunburn. Brett was there, nodding politely to everyone as they left, exhorting them to come again. When the tourists were all gone, she saw two other crew members assisting him, neither of whom was Bill Johnson. She jumped down from the car and made her way slowly over to Brett.

'Well, well.' Arms folded, he greeted her with a smirk. 'It didn't take the bride long to get bored with her new husband and come looking for me.' Deliberately, he took his time, looking her up and down, admiring her figure outlined in the bright, floral sundress she had bought in Port Douglas. Silently, she cursed herself for not changing into something less revealing before she left.

'Don't flatter yourself — I'm not looking for you, Brett.' She too folded her arms across her breasts, uncomfortable under his gaze. 'I want to talk to Bill Johnson.'

'I'll bet you do.' He laughed shortly. 'Sorry, darlin', the bird has flown. Told me some garbled story about killing your Dad and saying the cops would be after him. I didn't believe a word of it — thought he'd been drinking and imagined the whole thing.'

' 'Fraid not. He hit my father on the head with a shovel and knocked him cold.'

Brett had the grace to look concerned. 'Nasty. So how's your Dad? Is he going to be all right?'

'Apart from a bad headache and six stitches, yes.'

'No wonder Bill thinks he's a murderer.' Brett whistled softly. 'He said he was going to disguise himself and take the train north as the police might be watching the airports.'

'Well, they won't because Pa didn't report it. If it were up to me, I'd see Bill Johnson in jail. The police should be told and he should answer for what he's done. Unfortunately, Pa doesn't see it that way.'

'Bill was really freaked — scared of his own shadow. He had no money either and had to bot a hundred dollars off me before he left. He's gone for good this time, Leila. We'll never see him again.'

'I just hate to think that he's getting away with it.'

'He won't. Karma will catch up with him,' he said wistfully, subjecting her to that intense blue gaze that had once meant so much to her. 'Just as it did with me.'

She glanced at her watch, once more uncomfortable under his scrutiny. 'I should go. I have to get something for dinner.'

'Oh, quite the little housewife now, aren't we?' he said spitefully. 'Mustn't keep hubby waiting for his tea. Not when he's letting you drive his beautiful car.'

'Oh, stop it, Brett.' She turned towards the car, suddenly weary of his sniping.

'Leila — please. Don't go yet. I didn't mean — '

'To hurt anyone?' She glanced at him over her shoulder. 'You never do.'

'I've never stopped loving you, Leila. I would have married you some day.'

'Goodbye, Brett.' She wriggled her fingers without looking back this time. 'Thanks for setting my mind at rest about Bill.' She knew he was watching her every move as she climbed into the Prado, started it up and drove sedately away.

She arrived home to find the house deserted and everyone out at the stables. Much as she expected, her husband and father together with Terry were all standing admiring Starshine Blue. Tim, the security guard, had just arrived for his evening shift. A small man who somehow exuded an air of menace, he carried two businesslike revolvers, giving Leila the impression that he knew very well how to use them.

'Doesn't Bluey look wonderful?' Jimmy said, seeing Leila arrive and pulling her into his embrace. 'I don't know whether to be pleased or disappointed that he didn't miss me.'

* * *

The three days of the Christmas holiday were among the happiest Leila could ever remember, spent with the two people she loved most in the world. To repay the Fleets for the surprise reception they had been given on their wedding day, she invited them to a traditional Danish Christmas Eve dinner. This was for Jimmy's benefit as well because he told her Christmas at Bannerman's used to pass almost unnoticed — the daily care of the horses taking precedence over all else. Naturally, Clive and his daughter would disappear to socialize and spend the festive season in some luxury hotel but for everyone else it was 'business as usual'. This made Leila doubly determined to show him that Danes knew how to celebrate Christmas in style. She also invited Terry Bayliss to join them. The shy young man had not long left his native Adelaide and had not yet made many friends on the island.

The day before, she had sent Knud in search of an imposing Christmas tree which now stood in pride of place in the hall, adorned with their traditional tree decorations that came out of hiding every year. There were the Christmas hearts she had made as a child under her mother's direction; hearts made of interwoven red and white paper — the colours of the Danish flag. She also found an old set of Christmas lights in the shape of candles and made sure they were ready to work. There were old-fashioned china birds to clip on to the branches as well as other glittering baubles.

She also raided the attic to rediscover the Christmas 'nisser' — little figures that hadn't been brought out since she was a child. These Scandinavian relatives of English pixies or imps, wore Santa-like hats and clothes. Some she placed on the window sills, looking out, others clung precariously to picture rails and one she placed atop a bunch of mistletoe, hoping that, by bringing the mischievous little creatures out of retirement, they might bring luck and fortune to the household. Jimmy laughed when he saw them.

'Leila, they're great. I've never seen so many little Santas.'

'They're not Santas, they're Danish nisser and they're very capricious. You have to take care not to offend them.'

'Oh,' he said, looking at them with a new respect. 'And every one of them seems to be different. Did you make them?'

'I wish. They were made by my mother; she was pretty good with a needle.' Leila paused, looking at the imp she still held. 'We haven't displayed them since she left us — I thought it might upset Pa.'

'And it's not going to upset him this year?'

'No.' She gave him a quick kiss under the mistletoe in the hall. 'Because this year we have too much to celebrate and don't need to dwell on sad times. In any case, he's fully occupied planning his trip.'

'Ah,' Jimmy said, suddenly less than happy as he recalled the conversation he'd had with Knud earlier in the day.

'I haven't mentioned it to Leila yet.' His father-in-law had seized a quiet moment to confide in him. 'But it's possible I'll be away for as long as six months. Well, I want to travel around and see something of Europe while I'm there — it's hardly worth making the journey for less.'

'But six months!'

'With you and Leila together here, the stables will be in safe hands. But you're going to need a trainer's licence if Starshine Blue is to continue his campaign.'

'A trainer's licence!' He stared at Knud. He hadn't bargained for something like this, not at all. It was one thing to fudge enough paperwork to satisfy a near-sighted vicar but quite another to give false information to the racing industry. Even his driver's licence was still in the name of Kirkwood. Stifling a sense of panic, he started looking for an excuse. 'But Leila's your daughter. Doesn't it make more sense for *her* to put in for the trainer's licence, not me?'

'Stop being so self-effacing. You're family now as well as the stable foreman and I want you to be in charge while I'm gone.'

'Well, I'm flattered of course but I — '

'No buts. You and Leila can drive into town after Christmas and set the wheels in motion at least.'

In the face of Knud's determination, Jimmy could do little else but agree. Secretly, he promised himself to do no such thing. If another trainer's licence was really necessary for the stables, Leila should be the one to apply for it, not he.

Terry was first guest to arrive on Christmas Eve. Dressed in a red T-shirt and pink from the shower, his hair sitting up in short wet spikes, he looked not unlike a 'nisser' himself. Shortly afterwards, the Fleets made their entrance, dressed in festive attire and exclaiming at the Danish Christmas decorations. Then Tony presented Leila with a huge iced Christmas cake.

'I knew you wouldn't have time to make one,' Patsy said. 'And this one's Tony's speciality — full of cherries and booze!'

Leila thanked her and put it in pride of place on the big kitchen dresser, ready to serve later with liqueurs.

'But this is wonderful, Leila.' Patsy glanced at the nisser, smiling down from all corners, and the big kitchen table, set with a red cloth and many candles. 'If we weren't in the middle of a heatwave, I'd think we were in Denmark.'

'You're supposed to.' Knud smiled. 'The only concession to heat is that I'm serving champagne instead of traditional glögg,' he said, handing her a glass.

'Glögg?' Tony asked.

'Hot mulled wine with various spices and schnapps. Very potent.'

'It sounds it,' Tony said, also accepting a glass of chilled champagne. 'I'd like to propose a toast to the happy couple once more — to Leila and Jimmy. May their years together be long and happy and all their troubles be little ones.'

'Oh Tony, that's so corny!' his wife protested as everyone laughed politely.

'The best jokes always are,' he said, unrepentant.

Primed with champagne, all six sat down to a delicious meal served by Leila. She had cooked traditional roast pork with plenty of crackling, served with sweet and sour red cabbage and caramelized potatoes, knowing her father would expect it, but for Jimmy, and anyone else who didn't choose to eat meat, she had poached a whole salmon served with pickled cucumber and a fresh, green salad. Conversation flagged while they gave their undivided attention to their plates.

After the main course, crackers were pulled, disgorging paper hats and more silly jokes until even Terry relaxed and started to laugh. After this, Leila was ready to serve another Danish specialty for dessert; a dish of boiled rice swathed in whipped cream and vanilla mixed with chopped almonds and served chilled but accompanied by a hot cherry sauce.

'So simple and yet so sublime,' Tony pronounced, after tasting it. 'Do you mind if I add this to the menu at the bistro?'

'I'd be flattered.' Leila smiled.

Although by now they had all eaten their fill, even Terry who had managed to put away two helpings of dessert, they took a small slice of Christmas cake with a glass of Drambuie provided by Jimmy and which Knud hadn't tasted before.

'We had Drambuie every Christmas when I was growing up,' Jimmy explained. 'It was the only alcohol I was allowed to have.'

'And where did you grow up, Jimmy?' Patsy said, seizing the opportunity to quiz him. 'I thought you said it was somewhere in New South Wales?'

'That's right,' he said, easily. 'But I went to boarding school as a kid and even in the holidays, I didn't see much of my father — he was always too busy. I've always loved horses, so I made myself useful around the ranch. I helped to raise Bluey and took him to Bannerman's when I was nineteen.'

'Yes but where exactly was that?' Patsy was determined to pry.

'Jimmy doesn't enjoy discussing the past,' Leila said firmly, diverting her friend with a meaningful look. 'Who's for coffee?'

'Thank you, Mrs Jim, but I'd best be going.' Terry stood up with a glance at his watch. 'The horses won't sleep in, even if I do.'

'That's a good lad you have there,' Tony remarked when Terry had left, praising Leila's

Christmas feast and saying he wouldn't need to eat again for a week. 'Wish I could get kitchen hands that conscientious.'

'One in a million, he is,' Jimmy agreed. 'He thinks almost as much of Bluey as I do.'

Shortly after this, the party broke up, the Fleets thanking them for their hospitality and inviting them to attend a New Year's Eve Party at the bistro. Jimmy and Knud made Leila sit down to watch a film on television while they cleared the table and washed up. When they came in to look for her an hour later, Santa was still up to his antics on film but in spite of the noise and laughter, Leila had fallen asleep in the chair.

'Come on darling.' Jimmy kissed her gently, making her murmur in her sleep. 'Wake up and go to bed.'

Although they made and took meals in the house with Knud, they were still sleeping in Jimmy's cottage. Knud had already spoken of wanting them to move into the house at least while he went overseas but they still hadn't got around to dismantling and moving Jimmy's king-size bed. The truth was that, without wishing to hurt Knud's feelings, they preferred to sleep in a house on their own. Now they had been together long enough to have lost all inhibitions, their lovemaking had grown even more passionate and was sometimes noisy, as it turned out to be this Christmas Eve. The night was so hot and humid, it ignited their passions immediately until they came together with such hunger and ferocity that Leila wondered afterwards if they might be making a child.

'I've never loved anyone the way I love you.' Jimmy brushed a damp strand of hair away from her face as they lay in each other's arms, breathing heavily after their latest passionate encounter. 'Whatever happens, don't ever leave me, will you?'

'Leave you?' Her eyes opened wide and she stared at him. 'Why? What on earth makes you think I'd ever do that?'

'Nothing. Nothing, of course. It's just that everything fell into place so easily for us, I keep thinking something will happen to take it all away.'

'Silly Jimmy,' she murmured, closing her eyes again and giving him a languid kiss before allowing herself to drift off to sleep. 'We'll be here together until we are old and grey.'

While Leila slept the sleep of the exhausted, hugging the pillow, on the other side of the bed Jimmy lay staring into the darkness, his sister's words returning to haunt him. *Leila needs to know what sort of family she's marrying into. And you need to tell her — now.*

9

Although Knud had planned on leaving for Denmark soon after Christmas, his relatives wrote advising him to postpone it at least until the end of March because of the bad weather. And indeed, a look at the world weather channel on cable confirmed that most of Northern Europe was in the grip of ice and snow with more than one international airport closed.

Jimmy felt reprieved, imagining Knud would shelve the issue of an additional trainer's licence only to find his relief short-lived. His father-in-law had already sent for the application forms and was now urging him to fill them in.

'But you won't have to leave until April now.' Jimmy made one more attempt to dissuade him. 'And we're such a small stables. It makes no sense to pay for two licences while you're still here.'

'These things can't be arranged overnight. It'll take time. You'll need your birth certificate and references that will have to be checked. Ask Clive Bannerman — he's sure to give you a good one.'

‘Wait!’ Once more Jimmy choked on a rising panic. ‘It’s only a piece of paper, sure, but I’d so much rather Leila did this — not me.’

‘All right. If that’s how you feel.’ Reluctantly, Knud gave way. ‘But it’s going to be much harder for her to get the right references. With a glowing report from Bannerman, you’d have a walk-up start.’

For the rest of the day, Jimmy felt haunted by a persistent uneasiness that he couldn’t explain. Even a romp in the sea with Bluey was unable to lift his spirits. He couldn’t help feeling that something dreadful was about to happen, hanging over his head like the sword of Damocles. Even the horse was subdued, reflecting his sombre mood.

The six o’clock news provided the answer. Jimmy sat frozen, feeling the colour drain from his face as he sat staring at the screen as the announcement was made, the news-reader lowering his voice and looking suitably solemn:

> Multi-millionaire businessman, James Kirkwood, died last night when his private aircraft crashed into the sea off the coast of Queensland The cause of the accident is not yet known but it’s believed the plane may have been struck

> by lightning. Only Mr Kirkwood and his pilot, Jake Heron, were aboard and their bodies have not yet been recovered. Kirkwood, whose many business interests include the international Kirkwood Hotels and a blood-stock ranch in Northern New South Wales, is survived by his daughter, Sally, presently on her way back from overseas and her younger brother, James Junior, described by Kirkwood's staff as something of a recluse whose whereabouts are at present unknown. No doubt he'll come forward as soon as he hears of his father's death.

A grainy photograph, magnified several times, flashed on to the screen. It was of himself and Sally, sitting together on a fence at Kirkwood's Lodge. He could even remember when it was taken. Sally, a leggy teenager with her skirt tucked primly around her knees and he himself maybe ten or eleven. Even with the public school haircut, he was easily recognizable as his present-day self. Quickly, he picked up the remote, changing the channel.

'Jimmy, don't,' Leila complained. 'I was watching that.'

'Whatever for?' he said harshly, pretending

to give rapt attention to an advertisement showing on the other channel. 'Rich men getting themselves killed in light aircraft. What can it possibly matter to you?'

She stared at him, suddenly concerned. He had never spoken to her like that before. 'Jimmy, are you feeling OK? You've gone awfully white?'

'I'm fine,' he snapped, lurching out of his chair and heading for the back door. 'Just need a bit of fresh air.'

'Fresh air?' She stared at him in disbelief. 'But it's much cooler inside with the ceiling fan — there's a hot northerly blowing outside.'

Her only answer was the slamming of the back door.

After leaving some distance between himself and the house, Jimmy stood propped against a tree, breathing as if he had run a marathon and trying to collect his thoughts. This was something so totally unexpected, it had taken his breath away. His father wasn't yet sixty and had seemed so invincible, so indestructible, almost immortal. And that photograph, together with others, must be in the papers already. His secret would be out and there would be no hiding from his true identity now. As usual, Sally's instinct had been right — he should have told Leila the truth long before; it was going to be doubly hard to break the news to her now. After her mother's desertion and her bad experience with Brett, he knew how much she detested secrets and lies.

As if thinking of Sally had somehow conjured her, his mobile rang and he checked it, seeing that it was indeed his sister calling. He considered switching it off and avoiding the call but he knew that would only postpone the evil hour. Sighing, he leaned back against the tree, putting the phone to his ear.

'Hello Sal.'

'You've heard then? I can tell from your voice.' Her own sounded thick with tears. 'When are you coming home?'

'I — I don't know. I only just heard about it — on the six o'clock news.'

'Jimmy, you can't keep hiding and turning your back on me now. It's too late for that. I had no choice but to tell the lawyers where you are — they insisted. They'll be in touch tomorrow, if not before.'

'Dammit, Sal! Why didn't you call me first?'

'I'm calling you now, aren't I?' Her tone was brisk. 'You're not a kid any more, Jim. It's time to face up to your responsibilies — all of them. We are his joint heirs and the business needs both of us.'

'The business!' Unfairly, he took refuge in anger. 'That's all Dad ever cared about and it sounds as if you're much the same. The business doesn't need *me* — it never has. *Dad* never has.' He heard her break down in tears again and was immediately contrite. The news was so fresh, it was too soon for him to feel anything other than trapped by this twist of fate but now he remembered how Sally had loved their father. 'Sal, I'm so sorry. I didn't mean to upset you. I don't know what I'm saying — it's all too new. But please, please don't cry.'

He heard Sally blowing her nose. 'Just come home. I need you.'

'I don't know, Sal. I'm in the bad situation of having lied by omission to both my wife and her father. Indirectly, that's Dad's fault too. He was so scared I'd disgrace the name of Kirkwood by going to Bannerman's as a stable hand that he made me use mother's maiden name.'

'As I recall, that was *your* idea and you were happy to do so,' Sally snapped back. 'You can't blame Dad for all your mistakes, Jim. I advised you to tell Leila the truth before you married her but you chose to ignore it.' She waited for him to protest again but he said nothing, knowing it to be true.

'And while we're on the subject of your mistakes, there's something else you should know. Dianne Bannerman got hold of the story already and is telling everyone who'll listen that she was engaged to you and you've broken her heart by secretly marrying Leila. She's lining up several chat shows in Sydney already.'

'But that's ludicrous, Sal. I haven't even set eyes on the woman since I left Bannerman's.'

'And that's not all. She's building up the story by saying she lost your baby.'

This accusation left him speechless for a moment, his mind reeling. 'But Sal, that's absurd. Surely, you don't believe her?'

'Well, it does sound far-fetched but I gather she's pretty convincing.'

'Sally, I had a fling with Dianne when I first went to Bannerman's — I was only nineteen, for God's sake. We weren't together more than a couple of weeks. The foreman warned me off so I stayed out of her way. I was too scared of losing my job. End of story. She's talking of something that happened over six years ago.'

'Well, you'd better pray for a new story to break. The papers are having way too much fun with this one. Casanova Kirkwood isn't the half of it.'

'No! Can't you suppress it?'

'How? It's already out there. But if you can talk it over calmly and rationally with Leila, I'm sure you can get her to understand.'

'I doubt it. She had a bad experience with an unfaithful boyfriend before. It left her very insecure. What can we do? What do you think Dianne wants?'

'Money, I suppose. She's caught the scent of it and doesn't mean to let go.'

'Then give her what she wants. Let her have some.'

'And lend still more credence to her story? I don't think so. I'm coming to Melbourne tomorrow and we'll decide what to do about her then. See you soon.'

'Sally, no! Please don't do anything so — ' But she had already cut him off Cursing silently, he returned the phone to his pocket and started to walk slowly back to the house. The back door opened and Leila came running out to meet him.

'Dinner's ready; if you're feeling up to it. What happened? Are you feeling better now?'

'I'll be OK.' He pulled her into his arms and hugged her close so that she wouldn't see the worry and anguish in his face. 'Sorry I snapped at you earlier.'

'That's OK.' She pulled back a little to look at him. 'Are you coming down with a virus? You still don't look a hundred per cent.'

After dinner, which he scarcely touched, and to avoid any further news breaks on television, Jimmy insisted on watching a long drawn out tennis match on cable until he fell asleep in front of it. Leila then switched over to a late night chat show, surprised to recognize the guest as Dianne Bannerman, dressed to kill and made up to the nines, her hair arranged in a dark halo around her face. She was sobbing daintily, taking care not to smudge her eyeliner as she dabbed at her eyes.

'And when did you last see him — this heir to the Kirkwood millions?' the host prompted gently, hoping his guest wasn't going to break down entirely.

'Well, not since he got married, of course. And I wrote to him about losing the baby but he never replied. Ohh!' she wailed. 'And I love him so much. How could he betray me like this?'

Irritated by Dianne's obviously theatrical performance, Leila turned off the television and shook Jimmy's shoulder gently. He was fast asleep, looking exhausted, and she sensed that something was unusually wrong. Seeing him so quiet and preoccupied as they were preparing for bed, once again Leila tried to get him to open up.

'Jimmy, what's the matter?' she said in a

small voice. 'I've never seen you like this. Is it something I've done?'

'Oh, darling Leila, no.' He caught her in his arms, almost smothering her with kisses until she asked him to stop as she couldn't breathe.

'But something's worrying you, I know.' She wouldn't let the matter rest. 'Jimmy, you're not alone any more. I'm your wife now. If something troubles you this much, you need to share it. Is it something to do with the horses? With Starshine Blue?'

'No. The horses are fine — except we're losing Dreamy Princess and we shall need to find some new horses and owners.'

'Why? Dreamy Princess has been here for years and the girls have always been happy with us.'

'Knud says they're selling her now and the new owner wants her to train at Caulfield. The couple of two-year-olds aren't setting the world on fire and are being sold to a riding stables so, with Party Animal injured, that leaves us relying completely on Starshine Blue.'

'No wonder Dad thinks it's a good time to go overseas.'

They were silent for some moments both lost in their own thoughts. Once more Jimmy was wondering whether to take the plunge and tell Leila everything before she found out from another source. As usual, he couldn't think where to start. 'Leila,' he said gently. 'Are you happy to stay here on the island for ever? Or would you be willing to leave?'

'Maybe,' she murmured, smiling and letting her arm fall across his chest. 'I could live anywhere, long as I was with you.'

'Because there's something I need to tell you. The — the real reason I was upset tonight — you see, that man, the one who died today in the plane crash — he was my father. James Kirkwood was my Dad.' He held his breath, waiting for her to open her eyes and sit up to confront him, quizzing him about what he'd just said. But she didn't. Her even breathing continued and when he leaned closer to peer at her, he realized his confession had fallen on deaf ears. Leila was fast asleep. Only then did the first pangs of grief overwhelm him. Silently, he wept for the loss of his father and for the relationship they'd never had.

* * *

The following day Sally arrived in a chauffeur-driven limousine shortly before noon. The routine work of the morning was over and Leila was making chicken sandwiches and soup for lunch. There had been some thundery showers and for now the heatwave had abated. Knud looked out of the window, seeing the car arrive.

'Not expecting anyone, are we?' he checked with Leila, glancing down at his crumpled work clothes and muddy wellingtons. 'Well, if it's a prospective owner who can't be bothered to ring before turning up, they'll have to take us as we are.'

Certain it would be Sally, Jimmy's heart felt like a stone, heavy with dread. He had tried to call her several times that morning but her mobile had been switched off.

A uniformed chauffeur got out and opened the door for Sally who emerged just as the finishing school had once taught her, gracious as royalty. She was wearing a simple but expensive short black dress that clung to her slender figure and she carried a large Louis Vuitton shoulder bag. Her hair, the same dark brown as Jimmy's was pulled away from her face into a severe chignon and a pair of huge dark glasses concealed her expression.

'It's my sister,' Jimmy muttered, hurrying out to meet her before she could reach the back door.

'This place isn't easy to find,' she said. 'We had to stop twice to ask for directions.'

He greeted her, unsmiling. 'I wish I could say it was good to see you,' he said until he realized she was shaking and gathered her into his embrace. 'Oh God, Sally, it is good to see you.' His voice broke with emotion. 'Are you OK?'

'No,' she said in a hoarse voice without her usual confidence. 'But it's good to see you, too.'

'Sal, why did you hire a limo? Isn't it a bit — '

'Because I didn't feel up to driving myself, especially in Melbourne where I don't know the roads. And, in any case, what's the point of pretending any more?' She took off her dark glasses to show eyes that were no longer tearful but had violet circles beneath them, betraying anxiety and lack of sleep. 'Your wife is going to ask questions now and you'll have to tell her the truth. And I brought some of the papers, too — so you can see what Dianne's been saying.'

'You're forcing the issue. I wanted to tell Leila myself — in my own good time.'

'It can't wait.' She shook her head. 'Dad has left us in a mess, Jim. He was in the midst of negotiations with the owners of a casino. They need answers now.'

'How can I help you with that, Sal? I'm a horseman not a businessman. Even Dad was beginning to realize that — '

'I don't care. We need to show a united

front and take decisions together. These are heavy people and with the best will in the world, my husband and I can't deal with them on our own — '

'Hold on there — you said husband?' He stared at her.

'Yes, I did,' She said, lifting her chin defiantly. 'You're not the only one capable of getting married without family present. Robbie's one of our company accountants — I've known him for years.'

'An accountant,' Jimmy repeated, having a brief mental picture of a skinny geek with pebble spectacles, squinting at a computer.

'And he isn't a humourless nerd,' said Sally, reading his mind. 'He's kind and astute and I love him. But we can talk about me later. Right now, I want to meet your wife and her father.'

Leila, taking to Sally immediately as she looked so much like Jimmy, seated her at the kitchen table while she opened another can of soup and made enough sandwiches to feed everyone. Knud took some sandwiches out to the driver who wouldn't intrude, insisting that he should remain with his car.

After lunch, while Knud went to his office to make some phone calls and Sally excused herself to visit the bathroom, Leila tackled Jimmy about his sister.

'But she's a lovely woman, Jimmy. Not at all the business harridan you'd have me believe.'

'I never said she was a business harridan.'

'No, not in so many words but you let me assume it. And her clothes. Did you see that handbag? I know genuine Louis Vuitton when I see it. Her husband must be very wealthy indeed.'

Sally, returning in time to hear this last remark, broke into their conversation. 'As a matter of fact, he isn't. My husband happens to be a wage slave.' She took a deep breath. 'It was our father who had all the money — '

'Sally, please don't start this. Not now.' For the last time, Jimmy tried to stop her revelations.

'Yes Jimmy, now,' Sally said gently before addressing herself to Leila. 'Before I married Robbie Fitzpatrick, my name was Kirkwood. Does that sound at all familiar? I am the daughter of James Kirkwood.'

'James Kirkwood?' Leila took a few seconds to think it through until she remembered the name from the television programme with Dianne Bannerman. 'Oh. You mean the hotel magnate who died in the plane crash?'

Sally nodded, biting trembling lips to stop herself breaking down.

'Then,' Leila glanced from Sally to Jimmy and back again. 'if you're Jimmy's sister and his name is Flynn, he has to be that man's stepson?'

'No,' Sally said firmly, ignoring frantic signals from Jimmy. 'I'm nine years older but we still share the same parents. Your husband is James Kirkwood Junior.'

'I'm sorry? I don't understand.' Leila started to feel as if all the air in the room had been snatched away and her chest felt so tight, she could scarcely speak. 'If — if what you're saying is true, then there's no such person as Jimmy Flynn. I'm married to someone who doesn't exist.'

'No!' Jimmy said. 'Leila, please.' He tried to catch her hands to make her face him but she wrenched herself free, backing away from him.

'And Dianne,' she whispered. 'I saw her. She was on television last night, saying how you betrayed her. Only I didn't know she was talking about *you*.'

'I don't want you to listen to that,' he said. 'You must know it's all lies.'

'Is it, Jim? Like everything else in your life?' Suddenly, everything that had happened began to make sense as it all fell into place. The wedding that should have been a joyous occasion but had been too quiet by far. His reluctance to invite any relatives. His tension and rudeness to the press at Patsy's impromptu reception. Her husband was turning out to be a man of mystery indeed and just as deceitful as Brett Hanson. She must have a talent for picking them.

Sally, shocked by the extreme reaction her news had provoked in her sister-in-law who had been so open and friendly before, started doing her best to mend fences. 'Leila, please don't be upset. Surely, this isn't such bad news?'

'Which bit? That my husband broke somebody's heart to marry me?'

'Leila, think about it!' Jimmy was almost shouting now. 'How can it be true? I've been here living in Melbourne for almost a year now. When have I had time to conduct an affair?'

Sally laid a hand on his arm to calm him as she addressed Leila. 'And I'm sure you'll find you're legally married. My brother has been known as Jimmy Flynn for more than six years now and — '

'Oh, I know all about that.' Leila turned on her. 'But he still didn't think enough of me to trust me with the truth.'

'Leila, please.' Jimmy closed his eyes in anguish. 'You have to let me explain.'

'You don't need to. I understand the whole

thing perfectly now.'

'Perhaps, if I were to make us some tea.' Sally picked up the electric jug and went to fill it at the sink. 'We can all calm down and get things in proportion.'

'Mrs Fitzpatrick,' Leila snapped back. 'Please put that down. If there's any tea-making to be done in this kitchen, I'll do it. But I don't think a cup of tea is going to be of much use to me now. What I need is a good lawyer.'

'Well now, Mrs Flynn.' Sally could be just as haughty, drawing herself to her full height which was equal to Leila's. 'While you're so busy getting offended and climbing up on your high horse, you might pause to remember that Jimmy and I have just lost our father in terrible circumstances. Right now I need Jimmy in Sydney with me but maybe when you've come to terms with your anger and start to see things rationally again . . .'

'So now I'm a madwoman, am I?' Sparks were almost flashing from Leila's eyes. 'Get out! Just go now and take your deceitful brother with you.' She picked up a notepad and practically threw it at Sally. 'Leave an address and I'll send his belongings after him, including his king-size bed.'

'Leila, you don't mean this.' Jimmy closed his eyes as if he couldn't believe that his worst fears were actually coming true. 'You're angry now but you can't mean to throw away all we have.'

'What *do* we have, Jimmy, really? When our marriage and the life I thought we should have together is nothing but a sham?'

'That's not true. We found something good together and my love for you has always been real.'

'Jimmy, leave it.' Sally tried to take his arm. 'We have a long drive ahead of us and a plane to catch. Leila's in no mood to listen to you right now.'

Jimmy shook her off. 'I can't leave until we reach some sort of understanding.' He turned back to Leila. 'And, aside from everything else, what will happen to Starshine Blue?'

'I was wondering when you'd get round to that.' She regarded him with wintry, grey eyes, an ice princess now, through and through. 'He stays here, of course. Starshine Blue belongs to my father.'

* * *

When Knud returned after doing his office work, he found his daughter seated at the kitchen table, staring into space, the limousine and its occupants gone from the yard.

'Funny girl, Jimmy's sister,' he said

conversationally. 'Typical city woman, I suppose. Seemed a bit tense to me.' And when Leila made no reply to his observations, he looked around. 'You're a bit quiet and thoughtful today. Where's Jimmy? Out at the stables with Bluey, I suppose?'

'No,' she said in a trembling voice. 'He's gone with his sister to Sydney. I — I sent him away.'

'Gone off to Sydney? But for how long?' Knud screwed up his face to peer at her, for once less than affable. 'When you know I'm leaving for Europe in a matter of weeks?'

Leila's response was to burst into tears and it was some time before Knud could make sense of what she was saying. When he did, she was surprised to find he wasn't entirely on her side.

'I don't believe a word of it. Dianne Bannerman is an opportunist from way back and I'd take everything she says with a good pinch of salt.'

'But she said she was carrying his baby and she lost it.'

'Well, that's a bit hard to prove now, isn't it?' Knud shrugged. 'And, all that aside, what has he done that's so terrible? He omitted to tell you his father was a millionaire; a wealthy man. Well, I'll probably be a millionaire myself when my Aunt Ingrid dies.'

‘Small potatoes, Pa. Jim’s father was a billionaire. You’ve heard of Kirkwood Hotels?’

‘I dunno. Maybe.’

‘Well that’s our man. Hotels and casinos, fancy bloodstock ranch.’ Her lips twisted in disapproval, making her look older than her twenty-one years.

‘Oh? And why is that all Jimmy’s fault? I’m not surprised he was dragging his feet about telling you, if this is how you react.’

‘Pa! I thought you, of all people, would be on my side.’

‘I don’t want to take anyone’s side. But I’m surprised at you, Leila. I never thought you could be so lacking in . . .’ he clicked his fingers, searching for the word. ‘In empathy for those two. Aside from the issues of money and Dianne’s ridiculous claims — ’

‘Not that ridiculous.’

‘Ridiculous claims,’ Knud insisted. ‘Quite aside from all that, Jimmy and his sister have been most tragically bereaved. How would you feel if that suddenly happened to me? If I were to die in a plane crash on the way to Denmark?’

‘Don’t say such things, even in jest.’ Leila hugged him close. ‘It isn’t the same. Jimmy told me he has never been close to his father.’

‘But his sister was,’ Knud said softly. ‘So don’t punish her now for wanting her brother in his rightful place at her side.'

'Stop it, Dad. I can see where you're coming from. You're trying to make me feel as if I'm in the wrong — but I'm not.'

'Just think about it, Leila — with a cool head and an open heart.'

But she couldn't get over the feeling of being betrayed. Deserting the cottage with her husband's things untouched inside, she returned to her old bedroom in the house. She even locked up the Prado in the garage attached to the cottage, refusing to drive it because it reminded her too much of Jimmy. To begin with, he called from Sydney every day to see if she'd speak to him but she wouldn't even answer the phone, leaving Knud to take all the calls. And then, as if fate were being deliberately cruel, another disaster struck. Party Animal died.

The horse had been mending well and the vet was happy to let him walk on the beach and start working his strength up again. Terry and Ben set off with the two horses, Party Animal and Starshine Blue, meaning them to take a gentle canter on the beach. But instead of their local beach being deserted and completely their own as it usually was, there were a dozen or so school children playing there and preparing to run a race, a teacher brandishing a starting pistol, getting ready to set them off. Terry waved at him, signalling frantically for him not to use it but either he didn't see Terry or chose to ignore him. The starting pistol fired with a deafening, crack and Party Animal set back his ears and bolted, throwing Ben off as he did so. Terry, after making sure Ben was just bruised, rode Bluey in pursuit of the bolting horse who didn't look like stopping although he was headed for the rocks at the other end of the beach.

Just before he crashed into them, the horse seemed to falter and stop. Terry had almost reached him, stretching out to grab the big gelding's reins. But before he could do so, Party Animal staggered, gasped and fell heavily to the ground, blood pouring from his mouth and nose. Before Terry's horrified gaze, he twitched a few times and lay still. The young horseman didn't need to examine him further to be quite sure the horse was dead.

He arrived back at the house, weeping hysterically and, for a while, the Christensens found it hard to take in what he was trying to tell them. Knud clapped a hand to his mouth, believing at first it was Starshine Blue who had died but quickly hid his relief when he saw Leila's stricken face. Party Animal had been her project and her pet.

'Could you be mistaken?' She searched Terry's face for any sign of doubt. 'Maybe it isn't too late to send for the vet.'

'No, he's dead, Mrs Flynn,' Terry whispered, slowly shaking his head.

'So how did you leave him?' She glared at Terry until her father laid a restraining hand on her shoulder. 'Alone, like a dead thing washed up by the sea?'

'No. Of course not.' Terry looked shocked by her accusation. 'Ben's sitting with him until we can go back and fetch him.'

In spite of the fact that it was summer and the ground rock hard, she made Terry and her father help her to dig up half the old rose garden until they had a grave deep enough to bury him. Then she re-planted the rose trees, wearing black and weeping bitterly, as if she had lost a child. Within days after that, Dreamy Princess left for the city and Ben surprised Knud by asking if he could go with her. The two-year-olds also departed, leaving the stables empty apart from the lonely champion, Starshine Blue.

10

Having experienced one week without Jimmy already, while he was on honeymoon in Queensland, Starshine Blue didn't react to his absence immediately, content to make do with the attentions of Leila and Terry. But when this absence stretched from a week to a month and then six weeks, the horse gradually began to lose his good spirits and started to pine.

'I don't believe it,' Terry confided to Knud. 'Most horses don't care who looks after them, long as they're getting their creature comforts and regular feed. Bluey's not like that — you can see him losin' heart every day and he's never goin' to win any races for you like this.'

'He's missing Party Animal,' said Knud. 'Perhaps we should get him a companion, a pony?'

'Maybe.' Terry's plain, earnest features were creased with worry. 'Look, I dunno what happened between Mr and Mrs Flynn — an' I don't want to, boss. But before Bluey goes too far down, I think Jimmy should know how he is.'

'I think so too. I have the number but we'll make the call outside in the stables.' Knud glanced nervously towards the kitchen where Leila was washing up, clattering pans like a fury. She spoke only in monosyllables and seemed angry with everyone these days.

To begin with, he tried Jimmy's personal mobile, only to pick up a recorded message: *Hi, this is Jim. I can't talk to you now but if you leave a message after the tone, I'll get back to you . . .*

Swearing softly, Knud rang off and looked up the Sydney number of the Kirkwood's offices. He reached it quite easily on the landline but it was a different matter when he asked to be put through to Jimmy.

'Mr Kirkwood is in a conference and can't be disturbed,' an affected female voice informed him. 'Leave a message and I'll get him to — '

'I don't have time for your games, miss. I'm ringing from Melbourne.' For once Knud asserted himself. 'So be a good girl and put me through.'

'I'm afraid I can't do that, sir. It's more than my — '

'Job's worth! I know,' Knud snapped back. 'Just tell him it's about Starshine Blue.'

The line went dead for a moment but Jimmy was on it in seconds. 'Knud?' he said wistfully. 'Good to hear you. How is she?'

'Leila? In good form, making everyone's life a misery.'

'Oh.' This came out as a sigh. 'So she hasn't forgiven me yet?'

' 'Fraid not.'

'I was hoping — as she didn't send on my stuff, not even the car, that things might be thawing a bit.'

'I'm sorry, Jimmy, if my call got your hopes up but I'm not ringing about Leila. It's Starshine Blue.'

'God but I miss him. I miss all of you — the whole way of life. I've never been cut out for an office job. He's all right, isn't he?'

'At the moment, yes. But Terry's worried about him and so am I. Party Animal died of a heart attack recently and that's upset him as well. He's losing weight when he shouldn't and we think he's pining for you.'

'That does it. We're at a stage here when they can do without me for a few days — well, they'll have to — I've neglected him long enough. I'll be there tomorrow unless you hear otherwise. You and I need to have a serious talk.'

'Make it around midday if you don't want to see Leila. Tony Fleet's father died so Leila's been helping out, cooking lunch at the bistro. Not usually back until after three.'

* * *

Patsy had also been less than sympathetic when Leila recounted the events leading up to Jimmy's departure.

'Bloody hell, girl, what's wrong with you?' she said, taking it all as a huge joke. 'So the pauper has turned out to be a prince in disguise. I always knew he was hiding something but at least he isn't a career criminal or a fugitive on a witness protection programme. Hah! I wish Tony's father had been a multi-millionaire — you wouldn't hear me complaining then.'

'It's not funny, Patsy. Jimmy lied to everyone, not just to me. You do know he was engaged to a girl, got her pregnant and left her?'

'You sure?' Patsy wrinkled her nose, disbelieving it. 'He didn't seem like that sort of guy to me.'

'Believe me, Patsy. For most of his adult life, he's been living a lie.'

'Maybe he just wanted to make sure you weren't marrying him for his money.'

'Oh, I can't talk to you when you won't take it seriously.'

'Sorry.' Patsy sighed. 'But he married *you*, didn't he? Not that other girl. Honestly, Leila, I still don't see what the problem is.'

‘He isn’t the person I thought he was, that’s all.’

‘No. He’s someone better. Think about it, Leila. You could be living in a mansion on Double Bay, having weekly manicures and wearing Prada or Chanel to the races. And you’re tall enough to wear model hats; you could be one of those ladies who lunch.’

‘Ugh!’

‘You could even have a butler and a maid.’

‘I don’t want any of those things!’ Leila ranted. ‘I never did. I just want life to be normal — the way that it used to be.’

‘Ssh! You’re disturbing the paying customers.’ Patsy realized some of the people in the dining room were glancing nervously towards the kitchen.

‘Sorry. But it makes me so mad when people don’t understand.’

* * *

Jimmy arrived in a taxi just after noon the following day. Seeing him for the first time in two months, Knud was surprised to see the subtle changes that had taken place. Always slender, he had lost even more weight and there was a weary look about his eyes, making him look older than his twenty-five years. Jimmy had always worn good clothes but with a raffish, uncaring attitude and untidy, long hair. Today, he had abandoned the stetson and looked like a businessman on a day off, freshly shaved and with his dark hair neatly barbered. He was wearing a tie with a buttoned-down shirt under a tweed hacking jacket over well cut casual trousers and he carried a new, expensive-looking briefcase.

Knud clapped him on the shoulder and took him in a half embrace. 'Good to see you, son.' He glanced at his watch. 'But we'd better not waste any time. Three hours might seem long enough now but it isn't. Leila was home by 2.30 yesterday.'

'I'm not afraid to run into her. In fact, I thought of staying to see her when she comes back. We can't go on like this.'

'I don't know, Jimmy. I gather she's hiring some hot divorce lawyer but she doesn't say much about it to me. I'm accused of being on your side.'

Jimmy's face fell. 'I didn't think she'd be in such a hurry to be rid of me.' He shrugged. 'Oh well, no point in worrying about that now. Lets go and see what's happening with Bluey.'

As soon as the horse heard Jimmy's voice, he started whinnying and kicking the door of his stall. And when his old friend opened it and came in to see him, patting his neck and then pressing his forehead to the shooting star on his own, the horse snorted and pawed the ground as real tears gathered and spilled from his eyes.

'Well, I'm damned,' muttered Terry. 'I've heard that horses can weep but I've never seen it before.'

'What are we going to do?' Jimmy turned to Knud, close to tears himself, his voice cracking with emotion. 'I can't come back, even if Leila would have me, but I know I can't leave him again.'

'Let's go to the house and discuss it calmly over lunch.'

Hanging his jacket on the door to reassure the horse that he would return, Jimmy left Terry to feed him. Starshine Blue seemed brighter already and looked like eating with gusto for the first time in days.

Back at the house, Knud poured a glass of red wine for each of them and set a bowl of chunky vegetable soup in front of his visitor, together with a basket piled high with Leila's homemade bread.

'Oh,' Jimmy sighed, taking a piece. 'How I've missed Leila's bread.'

They didn't talk much while they were eating but afterwards, Knud made coffee for both of them and sat back, regarding his son-in-law with a sympathetic gaze. 'It's

1.15.' He nodded towards the kitchen clock. 'We've got just about an hour to decide what to do.'

'You don't think it wise for me to stay and see Leila?'

Slowly Knud shook his head. 'Not today. She was angry enough before but when she lost Party Animal, it seemed to push her over the edge. Patsy Fleet is the only one who can do anything with her. I'm sure I can't.' Knud cleared his throat to hide his emotion. 'It's not like her to bear such a grudge; as a rule, she's easygoing, like me. Look how she put up with Hanson for all those years?' He realized he had said the wrong thing as Jimmy frowned, not liking to be reminded of his wife's former love. 'But deep down I'm sure she still loves you and when she gets over the wrong she imagines has been done to her, she'll come around.'

'I wish I could be so sure.' Jimmy finished his coffee and Knud poured some more. 'Don't you want to ask me about Dianne?'

'Certainly not. Any fool can see that she's lying.'

'Any fool except Leila. She's the one who's been most hurt which is just what Dianne intended.'

'But why? Why would she do it?' A kindly man himself, Knud found such casual cruelty hard to understand.

'To get media attention, I suppose.' Jimmy sighed. 'Dianne has always longed to be famous just for being famous. My sister reckons it's best to ignore her. She'll give up when she sees she's not getting anywhere.' He gave a wry smile, changing the subject. 'And your trip to Europe. What about that?'

'Shelved until I know what's happening with Leila. I can't leave her here on her own. That's why the stables are empty apart from Bluey. I haven't told her yet but I'm putting the place on the market. I've not felt the same about it since someone broke in and gave me that crack on the head.'

'But you can't give it up — it's your home. You've lived here for most of your life.'

'Exactly. Which is why I want a change of scenery now, to travel and see something of the world before I'm too old to enjoy it. Jimmy, I've been awake half the night, thinking and planning ever since I spoke to you yesterday, but first there's something I have to know. I'm sure you're making a lot of changes in the shake-up after your father's death but I hope you're not thinking of selling Kirkwood's Lodge?'

'Hell, no.' Jimmy looked shocked at such a suggestion. 'It's the last thing I'd ever do. Going there for the occasional weekend has been the only thing keeping me sane.'

'Then Bluey should be there with you. He's given me a good season here and I don't want to see him raced until he breaks down. I think you should take him with you — now, today.'

'Today?'

'Why not? His horsebox is here and so is your Prado. I've been getting Terry to turn over the motor from time to time to stop the battery going flat.'

'Doesn't Leila drive it?'

'Not any more. She hasn't touched it since you left. Come on, Jimmy, we both know you can't desert Bluey again.'

'Yes, but what about Terry? With the stables empty, he'll be out of a job.'

'Take him with you. He has no ties here and he's been talking about wanting to see the Gold Coast. He's devoted to Starshine Blue — he's an honest lad and a better horseman than most. I'm sure it'll take him all of five minutes to pack.'

'My God, you cunning old devil.' It was Jimmy's turn to sit back, grinning at his father-in-law. 'Got it all worked out, haven't you?' Immediately, his smile faded. 'But what about Leila? She's going to feel even more betrayed when she finds out you're pulling the rug from under her, selling the only home she has ever known.'

Knud's expression hardened. 'Maybe then she'll come to her senses and realize she should make her home with the husband who loves her.'

Jimmy was silent for a moment, only now understanding how wide the rift had grown between the father and daughter who had once been so close. He felt sorry for it. 'I don't like it, Knud,' he said at last. 'We'll do more harm than good by forcing her hand. She could turn against both of us.'

'It's 1.45 already.' Knud pointed again at the kitchen clock.

'This is crazy. We can't make life-altering decisions in the space of half an hour.'

'Then what would you suggest? You go back to Sydney, letting that beautiful animal pine and die?'

'No. No!' Jimmy clapped his hands to his head. 'I will take Bluey. But only on one condition — that you let me buy him from you. By now he must be worth half a million at least, maybe more including his breeding rights.'

'Don't be ridiculous! I didn't pay a fraction of that amount to Clive Bannerman and the horse is another year older now.'

'Let me finish. Dad's will hasn't gone through probate yet but we don't expect any hitches and the bankers are being pretty lenient. Why not? They're making a fortune out of us, anyhow. Luckily, the casino deal wasn't too far advanced and we were able to back off without losing much money. Everything else is much more manageable without it. Ideally, I'd like my sister and her husband to supervise the management of the hotels while I look after the thoroughbreds — the horse breeding side of our enterprise.'

'That would work and it would suit you down to the ground. It would suit Leila too, if only she'd come to her senses and swallow her pride long enough to hear what you have in mind.' After listening to Jimmy, Knud could see how much he had changed. His son-in-law might not realize it himself but he had become much more decisive and business-like during the time he'd been away.

'It's so green and beautiful up there and most of it's still unspoilt.' Jimmy sighed. 'It breaks my heart every time I go home because I know how much Leila would love it.' He took a deep breath to regain control of his emotions and stood up to open his briefcase and take out his cheque book. 'I want to pay you half a million dollars for Starshine Blue.'

'Nonsense! I wouldn't hear of it, Jimmy. It's too much. Just take the horse and we'll work it out later.'

'No, let me finish. I want you to put the

money aside in a trust fund for Leila. She doesn't even have to know it's from me.'

'Of course she will,' Knud almost snorted. 'She knows she wouldn't be getting that kind of money from me.'

'Whatever. But it will give her financial security and independence without anyone forcing her hand. I still live in hope that she'll change her mind about me.' He shrugged. 'But if not, she can buy herself a place here and stay with her friends if that's what she wants.' While he was talking, he had been writing the cheque which he tore out of the book and presented to Knud who accepted it cautiously as if he thought it might bite.

'That's a lot of noughts,' he said, putting it away in his wallet. 'Thanks, Jim. I'll go to the bank tomorrow.' Once again he glanced at the kitchen clock. 'Not much time left. Lets find the leg wraps, pack up the horse for travel and give Terry the good news.'

It was, in fact, well after three before Jimmy set off on his long journey north, an excited Terry sitting beside him and Starshine Blue in the horsebox behind. To Knud's relief there was still no sign of Leila but the way Jimmy had dawdled, taking his time, he guessed his son-in-law was purposely delaying his departure in the hope of seeing her. But at last there was no further reason to stay and, with a final wave to Knud, they set off at a sedate pace, not speeding up until they reached the main road.

Back in the house Knud sat down at the kitchen table, realizing how quiet it was with everyone gone. The silence was so profound it was almost a noise in his ears. And, with the stables empty of horses, for the first time in years he had absolutely nothing to do.

⋆ ⋆ ⋆

When she left the bistro just before three, Leila didn't go home right away. Instead she took the highway leading to the city. On a recommendation from Val in the furniture shop, she had an appointment with a lawyer who dealt in family matters and who was particularly good at finding ways to dissolve unfortunate marriages.

'Amanda Cutter.' Val had pulled a face at the memory of her. 'I don't expect you to like her and her bedside manner is non-existent — if you cry, she'll throw a box of tissues at you and tell you to get over yourself, but she sorted my little problem in no time.'

'I just want a divorce — soon as poss.'

'Pity. Your Jimmy seemed such a nice guy.'

'Didn't he though,' Leila said, not without bitterness.

As she drove slowly towards the city still thinking of Jimmy, she gasped as she was overtaken on the inside lane by a metallic blue Toyota, pulling a horsebox. Surely that couldn't be him? No, her mind must be playing tricks, she told herself firmly. She knew very well that his car was safely behind the locked doors of a garage at Ocean's View. All the same, she speeded up, driving closer to the Toyota to get a better look until someone in a car behind angrily sounded the horn as she was swerving into his lane. And by the time she made her way through the traffic, already building up for the rush hour, the Toyota and the horsebox were long gone.

When she arrived at the modern city offices occupied by Amanda Cutter and her colleagues, she wished she had taken the time to go home and change. These city girls in their businesslike black seemed incredibly well groomed, not a hair out of place as they tottered along in their pencil skirts and shiny, black patent high heels. She knew she wouldn't make much of an impression on anyone, dressed in the crumpled clothes she had been wearing to work. But going home would have delayed her further and a glance at the clock reminded her she was already ten minutes late.

Ms Cutter, when Leila was finally shown

into her presence, was not amused. A bony, rather than slender woman in her early forties, she had dark hair, cut in a severe bob, and piercing dark-centred blue eyes that put Leila in mind of a wolf.

'I work to a schedule, you know.' Amanda glared at her watch. 'And you're over ten minutes late.'

'I'm sorry. But the car park was busy and I — '

'So let's not waste time on excuses. My next appointment is at 5.15 which leaves just twenty minutes of your original half hour.' She looked down at her notes. 'You're here about your marriage I see. Has it irrevocably broken down? I'm obliged to mention that you and your husband should try counselling before we set the wheels in motion for divorce. Unless you've already done so?'

'No. My husband has gone interstate. I haven't seen him for the best part of two months.'

'He deserted you then?'

'Not really. I sort of threw him out.'

'Sort of threw him out,' the lawyer repeated slowly, making Leila realize how feeble it sounded. 'Did you have good reason for this? Was he unfaithful?'

'I think so. I'm not sure.'

'Well, you'll need to be.'

'And he — he lied to me about . . . '

'Mrs Flynn, you'll have to do better than that. I have to tell you that finding your husband out in a single lie is insufficient grounds for divorce.'

'You don't understand. I'm not even sure that I *am* Mrs Flynn. He let me marry him thinking he was a horseman, a strapper, and then I found out that he wasn't — that he was the son of this millionaire.'

'Whoa, lets back up a moment. You're losing me.' Amanda Cutter leaned forward, peering at Leila as if she were some sort of loony. 'Are you saying you want to divorce your husband because he's a millionaire and he didn't tell you?'

'You're twisting my words — you make it sound crazy . . . ' Leila paused, seeing the lawyer's eyes roll. 'My husband is James Kirkwood Junior.'

'Kirkwood.' Amanda sat back and thought for a moment, tapping her teeth with a pen. 'Yes, I remember. The old man died in a plane crash.' A calculating look came into her eyes. 'Kirkwood Junior and his sister are the sole heirs. So, where does your husband stand in all this? Does he want a divorce, too? It'll make things a whole lot simpler if he does.'

'I haven't spoken to him. I don't know.'

Amanda sighed, looking longingly at the

silver box that obviously contained cigarettes. 'Mrs Flynn, your case is riddled with uncertainties and until you sort them out, I don't think I can help you.'

Angry at the woman's cavalier attitude, Leila stood up. 'Then I seem to have wasted your time and mine.'

For the first time Amanda Cutter smiled. It wasn't a pretty sight. 'I don't know your husband, my dear, but from your point of view I fail to see what the problem is — unless you have solid proof of his infidelity.' She glanced at her watch again. 'I charge by the hour or part of it. I'll send an invoice.'

'What for? You haven't given me any advice.'

'Then here it is. Stop behaving like a spoilt child and be grateful for what you have. If I were you, I'd draw a line under what's happened and make my peace with my husband before he changes *his* mind about *you*.'

'Thanks for nothing!' Leila made a sound that was something between a sniff and a sob. 'That's the same advice I've been getting from all of my friends.'

She drove home, tired, furious and vowing to let Ms Amanda Cutter reach the point of suing her before she would pay that invoice.

And then, as the journey was long, and she had nothing but the car radio for company, she started to think about the lawyer's advice.

Was she behaving like a spoilt child? Had she been too hasty in condemning her husband for concealing his background? And hadn't she herself been irritated by Dianne's theatrics? Everyone seemed so sure her claims were all lies. Patsy had been supportive enough in her way but she'd left Leila in no doubt of her views. Even Val, who never criticized or said much about anyone, had called Jimmy a nice guy. And he was. Surely he hadn't grown horns and an arrow-headed tail just because he went by a different name? And last, but by no means least, there was her father, who had so looked forward to visiting Denmark and now seemed unlikely to go because he wouldn't want to leave her alone. She cringed, remembering how he had borne the brunt of her fury and resentment. How selfish and self-centred she had been.

Unable to face the thought of cooking a meal and tempted by the cheery image of the fish and chip shop, she went in and bought enough for herself, her father and Terry. They wouldn't take long to reheat in the Aga. It was well after eight and dark by the time she reached Ocean's View and she almost missed the real estate agent's board that had been posted by the front gate: *Unique opportunity to purchase a piece of the island's history. Large, comfortable country homestead with four bedrooms, two bathrooms together with refurbished stables as well as a separate dwelling for staff.*

Furious, she read no further. She paused long enough to write down the time and after-hours phone number of the agents, gunned the car up the drive, bringing it to a screaming halt outside the back door. She snatched up the fish and chips although she was too angry to think of eating anything now and burst into the house like a whirlwind.

'Pa!' she yelled. 'Those pushy real estate agents have gone too far this time. have you seen the board at the end of the drive?'

'You don't have to shout, I'm here.' Knud came into the kitchen to face a white-faced Leila, ready to explode with rage. 'Where have you been? I expected you hours ago?'

'Never mind that now. I need to talk to those agents about taking away that board.' And she reached for the phone and started angrily stabbing some numbers.

'Oh,' Knud said. 'There already, is it? I didn't expect them to have it up so soon.'

Leila put down the phone and collapsed into a chair at the kitchen table, the wind suddenly gone from her sails. 'You knew about this?' she whispered. 'How could you, Pa? You just went ahead arranging the sale of our home and the business we built together. When were you going to tell me?' She glanced up at the blank face of the closed circuit television. 'And hey! Why is that monitor off? You know we have to keep a twenty-four hour watch over Bluey.'

'No, we don't. He's not there any more. We have no horses left in the stables.'

'Oh, Pa.' Her eyes filled with tears as she clapped her hand to her mouth, believing she understood for the first time why Knud might sell up. 'He didn't die on us like Party Animal, did he? Why didn't you call me? I knew he was pining but I didn't think it was that bad. Please tell me we haven't lost Starshine Blue?'

'No, no. Starshine Blue is happier than he has been for weeks.' Knud put a reassuring hand on her shoulder. 'Jimmy came today and he's taking him back to his birthplace — Kirkwood's Lodge in the Tweed Valley.'

'Jimmy?' At last she turned to look up at him. 'Jimmy was here today and nobody told me?'

'Well, no. I told him to go before you came back as I wasn't sure you wanted to see him.'

'But I *did* see him while I was driving to town. I saw the Toyota and the horsebox on the freeway. Although there were two people sitting up in the car so it might not — '

'That's right. I sent Terry with him. Jimmy's a busy man now and he can't devote all his time to Starshine Blue.'

Leila's heart sank. Her husband had come all this way and gone again, taking the horse without waiting to see her. Now he had his beloved Bluey, there was nothing to draw him back. And, what wounded her most of all was that she had absolutely no one to blame but herself. Beset by so many conflicting emotions at once, Leila burst into noisy and uncontrollable tears. Realizing tissues would be totally inadequate, Knud handed her a clean tea towel and sat beside her, patting her shoulder and letting her weep until she was all cried out, apart from the occasional shuddering sob.

'Oh Pa, I'm so sorry,' she managed to say at last. 'I must have been horrible to live with. No wonder you want to sell up and leave me.'

'I won't leave you, Leila. Not until everything's settled between you and Jimmy. He said himself that you can't go on as you are.'

'I — I saw a family lawyer today and she was abrasive and rude. She didn't tell me anything that I wanted to hear. Even so, she did make me think about where we are,

Jimmy and I. She said I should make my peace with him before he changes his mind about *me*.' Her eyes filled with tears again. 'Perhaps he's already back with Dianne?'

'I don't think so.' Knud smiled at her. 'Not by the way he was hanging around in the hope of seeing you. He didn't leave here until after three.'

'So you don't think I've ruined everything? I might still have a chance?'

'The only way to find that out, Leila, is to go after him. Go to Sydney and see.'

11

As Jimmy drove north, listening with only half an ear to Terry's excited chatter, he was trying to decide where to prop for the night. They had only just left Melbourne behind and it was already well after four. If Terry was willing to share the driving and they pushed on through the night, they could be at Clive Bannerman's stables some time in the early hours of the morning. By doing so, he could kill two birds with one stone — Bluey could have a break in his old quarters, and he would confront Dianne about her claims. It would be interesting to see if she would persist with her lies, face to face. Also he wanted to square things with Clive, hopefully before the old man punched his lights out. Clive had always been an old-fashioned patriarch and Dianne, his only child, the apple of his eye.

'What's goin' to happen with Blue when we get up north, Jim?' Terry broke into his thoughts. 'You goin' to race him again?'

'Probably not.' Jim shook his head, keeping his gaze on the road ahead. 'Kirkwoods' has never been a racing stables. Aside from that, I don't have a trainer's licence.'

'But you could get one?' Terry persisted. 'Bein' who you are, you can get whatever you want.'

I can have anything in the world, Jimmy thought. *Except what I really want. My wife at my side*.

'Give it a rest, Terry,' he snapped back more severely than he intended. 'Try to get some sleep before I need you to drive.'

'Sorry,' Terry mumbled, looking injured and turning aside, using his rolled up coat for a pillow and composing himself for sleep.

Just over the border, they paused to eat a less than satisfying meal at a roadside café serving an 'all day breakfast', which turned out to be a mixed grill of sausages, mushrooms, tomatoes and eggs, floating in a sea of oil. Jimmy pulled a face, murmuring something about cholesterol cocktails while Terry, always ravenous like most young men of his age, happily accepted Jimmy's sausages as a peace offering. Expecting the coffee to be as much of a disaster as the rest of the meal, they were pleased to find it strong and surprisingly good.

When they set off again, having checked that the horse was happy and comfortable enough to resume the journey, Terry took the wheel. But not for long. Jimmy was quick to realize that the lad's skilful horsemanship didn't extend to his driving and, after a couple of hair-raising experiences on corners when he feared they might all end up in the ditch, he took over again. While they changed places, Jimmy called ahead to Bannerman's stable foreman, Tom Kelso.

'Jimmy Flynn!' His old boss sounded pleased to hear from him. 'Of course we'll be happy to see you and old Blue.'

'Thanks, Tom.'

'How're you doing? Pretty good by all accounts. Could've knocked me down with a feather when I heard. Sorry about your old man, though. Nasty way to go.'

'Yeah,' Jimmy said, not wanting to dwell on the subject. 'Look, Tom, is Clive there at the moment? Or — or Dianne?'

'No, thank God. The coast is clear.' Tom lowered his voice. 'Clive can stay away as long as he likes, the grumpy ole bugger. Like a bear with a sore head these days.'

'Because of me and all those rumours started by Dianne?'

'Don't you worry.' Tom gave a bark of laughter. 'Nobody here believed any of that. If they'd bothered to ask me, I could have set them straight. But oh no, the tabloids were much happier with their story of the heartbroken, jilted fiancée.'

'So — er — where is she now?'

'I suppose you'd like to wring her stupid neck. But you're too late. The bird has already flown. She met this pop star over here doin' a concert in Sydney. Old and ugly as Mick Jagger but she didn't care.'

'Really?' With relief coursing through him, Jimmy started to smile.

'So what does she do but follow him back to London. An' now she's sayin' she wants to marry him — his fourth wife she'll be.' Tom seemed to find it a huge joke. 'So Clive has gone over to talk her out of it.'

Jimmy's smile broadened. 'Think he can do that?'

'Maybe. If the bribe's big enough. Good news for you though, isn't it?'

'The best I've had in weeks. Nothing changes around here, does it Tom?' Jimmy felt as if a load had been lifted from his shoulders. 'Be seein' you. Oh, and I've another lad with me, is that OK?'

'Sure. Long as you don't mind if he bunks in with you.'

'No problem. I don't know what time we'll get in — we're still a fair way out.'

'Doesn't matter — we're not goin' anywhere. Expect you when we see you, Jimmy — we can catch up then. Starshine Blue can even have his old room back.'

'Thanks, Tom.'

As it happened, they didn't set off from Bannerman's for another forty-eight hours. Jimmy had a long talk with Tom Kelso about the future of Starshine Blue as Tom had a lot of knowledge and good advice to offer about advertising the stallion's services at stud. Terry was round-eyed, totally in awe of the number of champions housed in this high profile stables.

'You've got a good 'un there,' Tom muttered, watching Terry in action, grooming the horse. 'Loves the animals and there doesn't seem to be a lazy bone in his body.'

'I hope you're not thinking of offering him a job, Tom?' Jimmy folded his arms.

'No, no, I wouldn't rob you,' Tom said and then laughed a little too heartily to be sincere. 'But if he ever gets tired of the Gold Coast . . . '

'You'll be the last to know,' Jimmy finished and moved on to the next stall where he gave a gasp of surprise.

'What is it?'

'This horse. It's amazing. The Christensens had a bay gelding just like him — Party Animal.'

'Well, look a bit closer — this one's not a gelding, she's a mare. Goes by the name of Chorus Girl. Lives up to it, too. She's never goin' to be a star.'

'The Christensens lost Party Animal. He had a heart attack and died.'

Tom shrugged. 'It happens. Doesn't do to get too fond of any particular horse.' He cleared his throat then, realizing that wasn't too tactful, given Jimmy's attachment to Starshine Blue.

'How does she race? Is Clive pleased with her?'

'Nope. But then there's precious little that pleases him these days. He's been tryin' to bring up a Melbourne Cup winner for years but it always eludes him.'

'Do you think he'd be willing to sell Chorus Girl? To me?'

'Now what would you possibly want with a mare like that one?' Tom stared at Jimmy in surprise, for the moment forgetting he wasn't dealing with a stable hand. His eyes widened as he remembered and his professional guile took over. 'Ah well, there's good bloodlines in her background or she wouldn't be here at all. I dare say Clive would be willing to part with her — at a price.'

'Come on, Tom. You've just told me she doesn't race well and is never likely to be a star.'

'Me and my big mouth.' Tom grinned ruefully. 'But we can email Clive in London an' see what he says. He answers pretty quick if there's money involved.'

Jimmy smiled, knowing he would buy Chorus Girl, no matter how outrageous the price. Maybe Leila would never join him at Kirkwood's Lodge and, if not, the mare would be a constant reminder of all he had lost but he felt it was something he had to do.

The following morning they received Clive's reply to Tom's email.

> You can let that rogue, Jimmy Flynn, take that mare off my hands. She's never been much use to me. If he wants to build up a stable of no hopers, who I am to quibble? Tell him he can call it a belated wedding present.
>
> You may or may not be pleased to hear that for better or worse I'm now related to the lead guitarist of a group named 'The Rotting Dead' — the noise they make cannot be called music. Dianne, the fool, is ridiculously happy and already in foal with my first grandchild — this time I hope it's for real! Long as it doesn't arrive with metal studs in its face and a ring in its nose! Not much more I can do here now — be seeing you soon! CB.

Jimmy burst out laughing again. 'And I thought I had problems? Poor old Clive.'

'Don't waste your pity on him.' Tom shook his head. 'He'll be back here in no time, making our lives a misery.'

'I'm sure,' Jimmy said. 'And Terry and I will make ourselves scarce before he does.'

So, after a hearty breakfast in Bannerman's staff canteen, Jimmy made a few phone calls arranging for Chorus Girl to be transported to Kirkwood's Lodge. He found Tom, told him about these arrangements and thanked him once again for his hospitality and advice. He then rounded up Terry, steered Bluey into his stall in the horsebox and set off on the highway, travelling North once again.

* * *

Although Leila would have driven to the airport at once to demand a seat on the next available flight to the Gold Coast, Knud persuaded her not to be so impulsive. He reminded her that her husband might well take his time driving north and not reach his destination for several days. It wouldn't do for her to arrive ahead of him. She saw the sense of this at last, reluctantly deciding to wait until he was back in Sydney where she would catch him at the head office of Kirkwood Enterprises.

Meanwhile, she drove into town to splash out on some new clothes. Aware of the pitying looks she had received from Amanda Cutter's minions, she had no intention of being caught looking drab. Patsy had begged to go with her. 'Oh Leila, please. I haven't been to town for ages and a second opinion is always valuable; you know how I love watching people spend money on clothes.'

All the same, Leila insisted on going alone. Away from the restaurant, her friend's taste often strayed too far towards the flamboyant fashions of the eighties. With Patsy aboard, she could find herself decked out in a jewelled fake leopard design over a pair of skintight, shiny red trousers all held together by a massive hipster belt. The very thought of it made her shudder. The look she wanted was sexy but ladylike and she preferred to search for it on her own.

In town, she found herself caught between seasons, the new winter stock just arriving and the last of summer's lightweight clothing being sold off. Bearing in mind that Sydney would be several degrees warmer than Melbourne, she sorted through racks of pretty summer suits and dresses being offered at half the original price. An hour or so later, she was completely discouraged. Being tall and with a bosom to house, she was a generous size fourteen, and everything she had tried so far made her look like either a disgruntled bridesmaid or worse, the mother of the bride. Stressed and exhausted, she collapsed on a small sofa outside one of the changing rooms and burst into tears. For someone who rarely wept, she had been doing an awful lot of that lately.

'Can I help?' She felt someone sit down beside her, putting a gentle hand on her shoulder.

'No, I don't think so.' Leila found a tissue and blew her nose, recovering quickly and trying to smile through her tears. 'I'm being silly, really.'

'Try me.' It was an elderly but elegant shop assistant, her grey hair swept up into a severe French pleat and wearing an old-fashioned black crepe dress with a white lace collar. She had dark blue eyes that were still beautiful as she gazed at Leila with motherly concern.

'I need something really special and I just haven't been able to find it.'

'An evening dress for a party? A special occasion?'

'Not really. A day dress but nothing matronly or dowdy.'

'For a job interview?'

'I suppose it is. In a way.' She laughed briefly. Wasn't she auditioning being the wife of a millionaire?

'And how much time do you have?'

Leila shrugged. 'Only the rest of today.'

'That should be time enough.' She sat back regarding Leila more critically now. 'I'd say you're a girl who works out of doors? By the sea or maybe with horses?'

'Both,' Leila gasped. 'Are you psychic or what?'

'No. It's just good observation. You have fine skin and you should take better care of it. It's just a little wind-burned from your work out of doors. And this . . . ' She gave a gentle tug of the thick, ash-blonde plait hanging over Leila's shoulder. 'This schoolgirl plait should go to give you a more sophisticated, modern look.'

Leila grabbed it, protectively. 'I can't cut my hair. I've worn it long all my life.'

'Then it's definitely time for a change. I'm Shirley,' her new friend said, taking charge and offering a card. 'Now, I want you to go up to the salon on the fifth floor. Ask to see Jamie — he's a miracle worker and I promise you'll like what he does.'

'But — '

'After that, you'll go back to the ground floor to see Judy on the Elizabeth Arden counter. She'll give you a quick makeover and sell you what you need. And don't look like that — it won't be expensive.'

‘But I’ve never used much make-up, I don’t . . .’

‘Everyone can do with a little help, now and then. Even beautiful girls like you.’

‘But I’m not — ’

‘Now then, we don’t want to hear that.’ Shirley cut short her protests as she walked her towards the lift. ‘And when you’re done you can come back to me and I’ll find you the perfect dress.’

Alone in the lift, Leila considered staying aboard until it reached the ground floor and fleeing from the store. Instead, she found herself getting out on the fifth floor and meekly showing the card that Shirley had given her.

An hour and half later, she scarcely recognized herself. Her hair had been skilfully cut to frame her face, softening her rather determined jaw line. Judy, the make-up artist had prescribed a tinted moisturiser to calm the colour in her cheeks and a soothing cream for her to use at night. Also she had shown Leila how to use eyeliner and mascara to make her eyes look huge, emphasizing their unusual grey-green colour. She returned to the third floor but was disappointed to find that Shirley wasn’t around.

‘Uh-oh.’ The younger shop assistant looked embarrassed when she asked after her new friend. 'Not Shirley again.'

'Why?' Leila said. 'Is there a problem? She seemed so sympathetic, so kind.'

'She does. She is. It's just that she doesn't work here any more. People have to retire when they're sixty. Store policy. Shirley was here for over forty years and just couldn't accept it. Turns up out of the blue and works till the floor manager spots her and sends her home.'

'Oh, but she seemed so confident. Sent me to the hairdresser and a make-up artist downstairs.' Leila flicked her newly shorn locks. 'Even promised to find me the perfect dress.'

'She'll have done that before she left. Let's check the holding rail.' The girl rummaged through a rail of clothing behind the counter. 'Here we are. Is your name Leila?'

'Yes, but I don't think I told her that.'

The girl shrugged. 'That's Shirley for you. Ooh!' she said, checking the label and price. 'Nothing the matter with her taste.'

The dress that Shirley had chosen for her was a grey-green, exactly matching her eyes. Beautifully cut and with a skirt that seemed to swirl as she moved, it had a wide belt to emphasize the slenderness of her waist, without drawing too much attention to her bosom. And, of course, it was a perfect fit. At the register, trying not to dwell upon its exorbitant price, she drew out her credit card to pay for it. This time it was an older assistant who served her.

'My oh my! You're in luck,' she said as she checked the bar code. 'This dress shows up at only half the original price.' She looked at the label again. 'Of course, it is one of last season's styles.'

'But it's so exactly what I want.' Leila smiled. 'Shirley found it for me.'

'Oh no, dear, you must be mistaken,' the older shop assistant whispered, her smile fading. 'Shirley hasn't been working here for some time.'

Leila said nothing further because it was all getting too strange. There had to be a rational explanation for what had taken place. Shirley had seemed so warm, so real; she could even remember the touch of her hand on her shoulder. But all the way home she kept wondering if somehow she had received a make-over from a ghost.

When she got home, starving and looking forward to an early supper, she saw two cars parked outside the back door. Seeing one was a Prado, for one heart-stopping moment she thought it was Jimmy's, but on closer inspection she saw it was black. She found Knud in the kitchen, leaning against the rail of the stove, somehow managing to look self-conscious in his own home.

'Prospective buyers,' he whispered, pointing at the ceiling. 'The agent is showing them round.'

'Already?' Leila frowned. 'I didn't think we'd see anyone before the weekend.'

'Apparently there's a lot of interest. The agent says we'll get more than the right price if we hold an auction.'

'But that means we'd have to get out sixty days after we sign.' She shook her head. 'I don't think we should rush into this, Pa. At least wait until I've been to see Jimmy. We don't know how things will turn out.'

'Everything will be fine and I'll be in Europe for summer there. You'll see.'

They could say no more as the agent was ushering his clients ahead of him into the kitchen and introducing them as Mr and Mrs Rayne. The husband looked like a farmer, still in his work clothes, his weather-beaten features creased in a smile. In contrast, his wife was dressed for the city in high heels and a figure-hugging black suit. Rayne approached and shook hands with Knud.

'Nice place you have here,' he said. 'Far as I'm concerned it pretty much fits the bill.'

'You always were easily pleased.' His wife scowled, looking round with a critical eye. 'If

I'm to be buried out here, it will have to be thoroughly modernized — especially the kitchen.' Her gaze settled upon the Aga. 'I'm certainly not cooking on that.'

Leila gasped. 'But the Aga is the heart of a country kitchen. It keeps the house warm all winter.'

'And stinking hot in the summer, I suppose.' Losing interest, the woman glanced at her watch. 'Come on, Roger,' she snapped at her husband. 'We have another appointment, remember? Don't want to be late.' And without bothering to thank anyone for their time or even to say goodbye, she marched out, leaving her husband and the agent to follow.

'I'll be in touch,' the agent said, hurrying after them.

'What a horrible woman,' Leila said when they were all out of earshot. 'I hate to think of her living here in our house.'

'I don't think there's very much chance of that,' Knud said with a wry smile. He peered at Leila as if seeing her for the first time. 'You look different. What have you done to yourself?'

'I had my hair cut. Don't you like it?'

Knud shrugged. 'I'll need to get used to it, that's all. Long hair made you different. With short hair you look just like everyone else.'

‘Then Jimmy won’t like it, either?’ She looked crestfallen.

‘Don’t mind me — what do I know?’ Too late Knud realized how much she needed his reassurance. ‘Jimmy will be so pleased so see you, he won’t even notice.’ He could only hope he was right.

* * *

Two days later, standing outside the offices of Kirkwood Enterprises, Leila wondered if she should have announced her arrival. The company owned the whole building and there was a constant stream of visitors coming and going through the revolving doors. Rain threatened, although it had held off so far. She was grateful for this as she had travelled to Sydney without a coat.

In the foyer, she consulted the list of tenants — nearly all branches of Kirkwood Enterprises — until she saw the executive suite was on the sixth floor. Heart thumping and trying to decide what to say to him after all this time, she took the lift and punched the button for the sixth floor. Just as the doors were about to close, another woman leaped into it, also punching that button and grinning at Leila.

‘Not often the elusive James Junior gives a

press conference,' she said, waving her clipboard. 'Hope they haven't started already. I'd hate to miss it.'

On the sixth floor, Leila was disconcerted to find the foyer a hive of activity. A small stage had been erected at one end of the room with a microphone stand and chairs had been set in front of it, most of them already occupied. Leila glanced at the reception desk but saw that the two girls behind it were busy fielding enquiries. She hesitated, wondering what to do. Should she announce herself or not? Maybe she should just give up and come back tomorrow? While she was thinking about it, a PA came up and asked her to sign herself in. Absent-mindedly, she did so, adding her name to the list of visitors.

'Mr Kirkwood and his sister will be flying to Hong Kong tomorrow,' she overheard a businessman being told. 'You can leave your proposals with us today but he won't have time to look at them until he comes back.' This wasn't what the businessman wanted to hear and he snapped something back at her. An almost hysterical note crept into the girl's voice as she answered him. 'No, no I'm sorry. I've been told not to make any appointments until the week after next. I can't help it if that sounds unreasonable but . . . '

Not waiting to hear any more, Leila took one of the remaining seats at the back of the foyer, deciding to sit back and watch. She would wait until the conference was over and all these people had left. There would be time enough to announce her presence then. The woman who had accompanied her in the lift sat down beside her.

'Deirdre Curtis,' she said, introducing herself. 'From *Get The Buzz*. And you are?'

'Leila Flynn.'

'Representing?' The girl scanned Leila for a name tag, frowning when she didn't see one.

'Me? No one.'

'Ah. You're a freelance.'

'No, you don't understand. I — '

Her explanation was cut short as a tall, grey haired man took the stage.

'Ladies and gentlemen, welcome to Kirkwood Enterprises.' He smiled at his audience. 'Good to see so many people here. I'm Rob Fitzpatrick, Finance Director of our company. I have little to do here today except introduce you to the man you're all waiting to meet — James Kirkwood Junior!'

Jimmy had been fighting a thunderous headache all day; it affected his vision so badly, he could hardly see. Like a migraine, it had come on this morning when he boarded a plane and, in spite of hefty painkillers, had refused to be shifted all day. He had always hated flying — even more so since the death of his father — but in order to be here in time for the press conference, he'd had to take a commercial flight from Coolangatta. He had spent too long settling Bluey and Chorus Girl into their new quarters and making sure Terry was liked and accepted by the other lads. Kirkwood's Lodge always felt so much like home, he was always reluctant to be dragged back to Sydney, the hub of his father's enterprise.

Although he had made some progress in helping Sally and her husband to fill their father's shoes, public speaking still horrified him, especially the prospect of facing a motley collection of journalists who might well be out to 'get him' or, at the very least, make him look a fool.

To begin with, it was all right. Their questions were courteous and mostly concerning the changes that he and Sally had already made to the business and their plans for the future. After that, Sally and Rob were congratulated on their marriage with a rousing cheer but, as it died down, a woman stood up at the back, waving to get his attention and fixing him with a determined look.

'Deirdre Curtis — *Get The Buzz*,' she introduced herself. 'Tell me, are *you* still married, Mr Kirkwood? Or is there some hope for us single girls?'

'Married?' he whispered, shading his eyes from the bright lights, trying to focus on the woman who appeared as a distant blur at the back of the room. 'Yes.'

'Sorry, we didn't catch that?'

'Yes.' He cleared his throat to say louder. 'Yes, I am.'

'And what do you think of your former fiancée, Dianne, getting married to that musician?'

'I have nothing to say.' Jimmy looked desperately towards Sally, hoping for rescue but she was far away on the other side of the room. 'Would you confine your questions to business, please.'

'Bear with me.' Deirdre's eyes glittered. 'So, when are we going to meet the mysterious Mrs Kirkwood? Is she here with you today?'

'No. No — she . . . ' Once more Jimmy was floundering. Leila took a deep breath, preparing to stand up and announce herself until Deirdre spoke up again.

'Because rumour has it that you are estranged. That she's still living in Melbourne while you spend your time between here and the Gold Coast. She's even consulted a lawyer about a divorce. Would you like to comment on that?'

Fortunately, Rob was quick to realize that Jimmy was in trouble with this journalist and came to his aid. 'I'm sorry, ladies and gentlemen, but we're out of time.' He spread his arms wide, already shepherding them towards the door. 'Thank you for your attention but that's all for today.'

There was a concerted groan from those who had wanted to ask more questions, a few of them glaring at Deirdre Curtis who seemed pleased with herself over the minor drama she had caused. They knew she thrived on rumour and wouldn't hesitate to invent something to fill the gaps in her knowledge.

At last nearly everyone had gone apart from one woman still seated in shadow in the back row.

'Sorry, miss, but that includes you,' Rob called out to her. 'You have to be going now.'

Leila stood up slowly, realizing it had all been in vain. The make-over, the journey and even the dress all seemed laughable now. She shouldn't have come. Her Jimmy, the one she had known and loved, just didn't exist any more. He had moved on, swallowed up by Kirkwood Enterprises just as his father had always meant him to be. This man with his neatly cropped hair and Armani suit was a stranger to her.

Blinded by a sudden rush of tears, she hurried towards the bank of lifts, pushed into one and, without waiting for anyone else, punched the button for the ground floor. There she asked the girl on the front desk to call her a cab to take her to the airport. They owed her that much at least.

* * *

As the ordeal of public scrutiny was now over, Jimmy's headache began to recede although he knew he would have to give himself to the specialists and take some more tests. Once rare, these headaches were increasing in frequency now. Ready to leave with Sally and Rob, he stopped dead in his tracks. He could smell Leila's perfume — here at the back of the room. Surely she couldn't have been here? And, if so, why hadn't she waited to see him?

'Sally!' He whispered urgently, pulling his sister to his side. 'Can you smell that?'

'Mm yes. Givenchy,' she said, closing her eyes. 'Lovely.'

'It's Leila's perfume. She wears it all the time. Even out with the horses. If she came all this way — why didn't she stay to see me? And where is she now?'

'Oh, Jimmy.' She patted his shoulder. 'It's a

popular perfume. Lots of girls wear it.'

'No. It smells differently on everyone — Leila told me. And that's how it smells on her. I'd recognize it anywhere.'

'Oh, Jimmy.' Sally's smile faded. She was still feeling guilty and somewhat responsible for her brother's marriage problems. 'It can't possibly . . . '

'Just humour me, Sal. Show me the list of people who signed in for the press conference'

'All right.' Sally handed it to him reluctantly. 'But I don't think you'll find — '

'No, I'm right! She was here. There's her signature — Leila Flynn. Oh God, something must have frightened her off. That awful Curtis woman and what she was saying. I have to find Leila and catch her before she leaves.'

Having ascertained from the girl at reception that a cab had been called to take a Mrs Flynn to the airport, Jimmy rushed outside, hoping against hope that she might still be waiting for it. At this time of day, there were plenty of cabs in the street but no Leila. He hailed one himself.

'Airport,' he said tersely. 'Quick as you can.'

'I don't risk my licence for anyone.' The driver scowled at him. 'I don't speed and I never run any lights. It'll take as long as it takes.'

Although it seemed to Jimmy that the cabbie was being deliberately cautious, they were soon at the airport. Departures was busy and he scanned the constantly moving list, looking for flights to Melbourne.

'Please, oh please let me find her!' He was almost praying out loud. He ran the length of the airport, looking in every lounge until he realized a flight for Melbourne was actually boarding, the passengers forming a queue, getting ready to board. And then he saw her, lining up with the others. For a moment, he wasn't sure — this girl had short hair — and then he recognized her distinctive, loping walk.

'Leila!' he called out, hoping she would hear him above all the music and general noise common to a busy airport. 'Leila, wait!'

Focusing on the woman he so desperately wanted to stop from boarding that plane, he started to run towards her instead of looking where he was going. He tripped over somebody's luggage and crashed to the ground, striking his head on a bench as he fell. For most people, such an accident would be no more than an embarrassing mishap. This wasn't the case for Jimmy. He sat up cautiously, realizing with a sense of panic that the world around him was totally and uncompromisingly black. He could hear people talking to him and knew he was conscious because he could answer them. But he could no longer see.

12

All the way to the airport, Leila scrubbed away tears, silently cursing herself for being so naïve. She had come to Sydney with such high hopes only to have them all dashed. Even without speaking to Jimmy, she could see how much he had changed. He had moved on already, leaving her far behind. And, if that weren't enough, she had been shocked to find out how easily her privacy had been invaded. There must be spies everywhere. How else could a Sydney gossip columnist possibly know that she had consulted a lawyer about a divorce? She would have sharp words with Ms Amanda Cutter when she got back to Melbourne. If nothing else, it would be satisfying to catch that cruel woman on the wrong foot, making her squirm. Then she had a less happy thought. How was she to break the news of her failure to Pa? Pa, who was mentally halfway to Denmark by now, believing her future was settled. Unable to face talking to him directly, she sent him an SMS to say she was leaving Sydney at once and would shortly be home. That terse message would be enough to let him know things hadn't gone as he expected.

At the airport she found she could get a seat on a flight to Melbourne, leaving in less than an hour. Waiting in line to board the plane, momentarily she looked back across the room, thinking she heard someone call her name. But she was mistaken. She could see only strangers going about their own business. No one was waving to get her attention and, apart from a bunch of people gathering around a pile of luggage, nothing unusual seemed to be happening at all. Sighing, she smiled wearily at the girl at the counter and hurried on down the passage to board the aircraft and take her seat on the plane.

By the time she arrived in Melbourne, she had received a message from Knud to say he would be there to meet her and drive her home. Of course, with the stables empty, time hung heavily on his hands as there was little for him to do. She bought a magazine and sat outside on a bench to wait for him, preferring fresh air and the scents of autumn to the noise and bustle of the terminal, but she didn't have to wait for long. He greeted her with a hug, quick to interpret her solemn expression.

'I'm so sorry, Leila,' he said as he picked

up the small overnight bag which had never been needed. 'I must've read him wrong. I could have sworn he wasn't looking for a whole olive branch — a single leaf would have been enough.'

She shook her head, fighting tears. 'I never even got to speak to him, Pa,' she said, knowing how lame it would sound. 'It was so obvious that he's changed and moved on.'

'How can you possibly know that!' Exasperated, Knud paused on the way to the car park to stare at her in amazement. 'Leila, it makes no sense. How could you go there especially to see him and then bottle out?' He opened the car and threw her bag on the back seat and then got into the driver's seat, waiting for her to explain.

'It wasn't like that.' Miserably, she stared at her hands, unwilling to meet his gaze. 'When I arrived the place was alive with people. They were having a press conference and everyone seemed so busy. Then I heard someone say Jimmy would be flying to Hong Kong the next day. I realized then it was hopeless, so I left.'

'I don't believe this, Leila. Are you telling me you were actually in the same room with him and you didn't speak to him?'

'You don't understand. It was crowded and he didn't see me. And — and he looked so different in a suit and tie. So distant and unreachable. Not like my Jimmy at all.'

'Really? And you are not his Leila just because you've had your hair cut and are wearing a new dress?' Knud let go a gusty sigh. 'So where does that leave us now? D'you want me to take Ocean's View off the market?'

She shook her head. 'No. I haven't the heart to start over again with new horses. Not right now, anyway. I want you to go ahead with your travel plans. I can always move in with Patsy while I decide what to do. She needs me, at least while Tony's in Queensland looking after his mother.'

'But you can't waste yourself as a kitchen hand. You can't turn your back on the horses — they have always been part of your life.'

'I know. But there'll never be another Party Animal.'

'I warned you about getting too close to one horse. You lost him and it hurt. Jimmy's exactly the same about Starshine Blue.'

Leila glanced at her father, struck by a sudden thought. 'Yes Pa, what about Starshine Blue? You had all his papers when you bought him from Clive. So why did you give him to Jimmy?'

'I didn't.' Knud hesitated uncomfortably, wondering whether to say more. Finally, he decided it was time to tell her the truth. 'If you must know, Jimmy paid for him — very handsomely too. Half a million dollars.'

'What?' Leila considered this for a moment, stunned by this news. 'Oh, come on! Bluey's a nice enough horse but never worth that sort of money. He's nearly at the end of his racing days, too.'

'Exactly what I said to Jimmy. But he made me take the money to put in a trust fund for you. To give you some independence, he said. So there it sits — in your name whenever you need it. Half a million dollars.'

She stared at him, horrified. 'But Pa! Why didn't you tell me before?'

'I dunno.' Knud shrugged, keeping his eyes on the road. 'You didn't ask.'

'Because this changes everything. This is more than just recompense for Bluey. By making you take that money to open a trust fund for me, he's paying me off. I can expect divorce papers hard on the heels of this. Especially now he knows I've been seeing a lawyer myself.'

'Leila, don't jump to conclusions. That was not his intention, I'm sure. When I saw him last, he still hoped to mend matters between you. He told me that if only you could see it, you'd fall in love with the Tweed Valley ranch.'

'But I never will see it now, will I? We've drifted too far apart.'

* * *

Although Jimmy tried to prevent it, asking the ground staff to use his mobile to call his sister, they called an ambulance instead. When the paramedics arrived, he tried to make little of his failing vision, telling them it had always been temporary before. Ignoring his pleas, they took him to the casualty department of the nearest hospital. It was there that Sally caught up with him later.

'Sal, I'm so sorry.' Blindly, he reached for her hand. 'I don't think I'll be fit to travel with you tomorrow.'

'Nobody's going anywhere — we've cancelled the trip.' She squeezed his hand to reassure him. 'Rob and I won't be leaving you while you're like this. He would have come with me now but he's making sure nobody leaks the story to the press. The shareholders got a bad attack of the jitters when Dad died. It would be just as bad for business if they were to find out you're sick.'

'Sal, I promise you I'm not sick. They're making a fuss about nothing. It's happened before and my eyesight always comes back.'

'Well, Jimmy, I hope so. But I have to tell

you they're not too happy about it here.'

'What do they know? Young doctors, fresh out of med school.'

'They know a hell of a lot more than you do.' Anxiety made Sally waspish. 'They're suggesting I move you to a private hospital where you can get specialist help.'

'No, Sal, I don't need it. Why can't I go home? I'll be OK in the morning after a good night's sleep.'

'And what if you're not? Jimmy, how many of these attacks have you had and over what period of time?'

'They're not attacks. Usually, they follow an accident of some sort.'

'How many times? Tell me.'

'I dunno. Once or twice.'

'What makes you think I don't know when you're lying?' she snapped.

'Sally, I can't remember. It hasn't happened for some time.'

'So the first episode was some time ago?'

'All right — yes. When I was at Bannerman's. I had a fall during track work and he paid for me to see an eye specialist and a neurologist — a Dr Wilson Stewart.'

'Finally,' Sally said, moving off his bed.

'Where are you going?'

'To get you into a hospital where you can see Dr Wilson Stewart.'

'Sally, please! No!'
But he knew she had already gone.

* * *

Leila dressed with care before going to see Ms Amanda Cutter again. Also she made sure she was early for her appointment, looking forward to complaining if there was any delay. She was almost disappointed when she was shown into the woman's office on the tick of half past four.

'Well, Mrs Flynn.' The lawyer regarded her, head on one side. 'I hope you've brought me something I can get my teeth into this time?'

'Maybe.' Leila was equally cool. 'But first I have a matter to raise with you concerning the confidentiality of my case.'

'Go on.' The lawyer sat back regarding her, her expression becoming more and more serious as Leila explained what had happened in Sydney. She stood up as soon as she finished.

'Will you excuse me for a moment? In view of what you've just told me, I need to speak to my staff.'

'Certainly,' Leila said, straining her ears but failing to hear what was said in the outer office although someone burst into noisy hiccupping sobs. In less than five minutes, Ms Cutter was back.

'New clerical assistant. Thought she'd make some pocket money by leaking stories to the press. Sorry about that.'

'And that's it, is it? You're sorry?'

Amanda shrugged. 'What more can I do? I've given the girl the sack.'

'But my husband now knows that I'm seeing a lawyer.'

'So? He'll know soon enough, anyway, when we set the wheels in motion for your divorce. You should do very well, Mrs Flynn.' Once more a calculating look came into the lawyer's eyes. Leila could almost hear the cash register clanging. 'If we can prove infidelity with his former fiancée as well as mental cruelty and desertion, I should be able to get you three million at least — maybe more.'

'But I don't want his money.' Leila whispered, appalled. 'He's already put half a million in trust for me — I don't even want that.'

'What did you say?' Amanda glared at her. 'Of all the stupid . . . You've accepted money from him? Don't you realize that can prejudice your case?'

Leila stood up, drawing herself to her full height so that she towered over the lawyer, seated at her desk. 'Ms Cutter, I didn't come here for your advice. I came to complain of a breach of confidentiality on the part of you or your staff. And if I do find myself in the midst of divorce proceedings, I don't think I'd want you to act for me, after all.'

'Why ever not?' Amanda's face went brick red with temper as she saw the juicy retainer and commission sliding from her grasp. 'I have the reputation of making more money for my clients than any other divorce lawyer in town.'

'I told you before,' Leila said softly. 'I'm not interested in my husband's money.' And she left the room, closing the door very quietly behind her.

* * *

'You've done well, Mrs Fitzpatrick.' A small man in his forties, neatly dressed and with a kindly expression in his eyes, Wilson Stewart regarded her, smiling. 'Your brother ought to be grateful for your care. Had you not taken charge and convinced him to see me, it could have been much worse. As it is, there is only a fifty-fifty chance that his eyesight can be fully restored.'

'He says it always came back on its own before.'

'Yes. It is amazing how the human body can adjust but, unfortunately in his case, not any more. How long is it since the original accident?' He looked down, scanning his notes. 'Yes. Nearly six years ago. I told him to come to Sydney for follow-up visits and scans as I should need to monitor his progress over several years. But he cancelled his next appointment and never came back.'

'That sounds like Jimmy.' Sally smiled ruefully. 'Never trouble trouble.'

'Well, he's got trouble enough now in the form of a brain tumour.'

'Oh no!'

'Sorry. I shouldn't have broken the news like that. It may not be as alarming as it sounds but I'm referring him to a colleague who is a neurosurgeon — a Mr Duncan Browne. The tumour needs to be removed and soon.'

'But Jimmy has never had surgery in his life. He's always hated the idea.'

'Without it, the tumour will continue to grow and the symptoms will only get worse.'

'But afterwards — he will be well again? His eyesight can be fully restored?'

'Hopefully, yes.'

'Only hopefully?'

'Let's not dwell on the worst until it has happened, Mrs Fitzpatrick. Now you are his next of kin, aren't you? His immediate family?'

'Yes. Yes, I think so. James is married but he and his wife are estranged. She's living in Melbourne.'

'Estranged or not, she should be informed of the seriousness of his condition. Post-operatively, he will go through a tough time while we wait to see if the surgery has been successful. He's going to need all the support he can get.'

⋆ ⋆ ⋆

This was the last day that Knud and Leila would spend together at Ocean's View. Knud had accepted a handsome offer for the house and adjoining stables from people they knew and liked. Tina Blacklock, whose father owned a riding school on the Peninsula, was soon to be married. She and her husband wanted to establish a second riding school on the island for the benefit of the locals as well as organizing pony trekking for the tourists. Knud and Leila were delighted that Tina and her new husband would be taking over their home. People who would appreciate the history and character of the old place and were content to take it as it was, complete with the rather old-fashioned furniture and fittings.

Tomorrow, Leila would move in with Patsy while Knud flew to Amsterdam where he was to begin his European adventure. So far as future plans were concerned, they would consider their options when he came back. Secretly, Knud still cherished a hope that his daughter and her husband would find a way to resolve their difficulties and get back together. They were meant for each other, he was sure of it and neither would be happy with anyone else.

So they looked at each other in surprise when mid-afternoon there was a knock at the back door.

'Not expecting anyone, are we?' said Knud, looking out of the window. 'Don't recognize the motor — looks like a hired car.'

Leila opened the back door, far from pleased to see her sister-in-law standing there. 'What can you possibly want from me now?' she snapped. 'Why are you here?' More than impolite, she knew she was being downright unfriendly but she couldn't help feeling that Jimmy's sister was the catalyst of all her woes. Today Sally looked drawn and harassed, wisps of hair hanging down from her usually immaculate French pleat.

'Now Leila, that isn't kind.' Gently, Knud reproached his daughter who was still glaring at Sally without inviting her in. 'Come in and sit down Mrs — er — Fitzpatrick, isn't it? Can I offer you coffee? Or would you prefer something stronger?'

'Thank you, coffee will be fine.' Relieved to be asked to take a seat, Sally almost collapsed at the kitchen table, her head in her hands, making Knud shake his head and frown at his daughter. And when he placed a cup of steaming coffee in front of Sally, she looked up at him with a weary smile. She took a few sips before going on.

'I don't really know where to start,' she said, sitting back and looking at her sister-in-law who was sitting bolt upright, regarding her with a glacial expression An ice princess, indeed, Sally thought.

'Take your time,' Knud said. 'You wouldn't have come all this way if it wasn't important.'

'You're right, I wouldn't. And it is.' She took a deep breath as tears threatened. 'You were in Sydney, weren't you, Leila? At our press conference?'

'Yes.' Leila stared at her in surprise. 'But how did you know?'

'For one thing, you signed the visitors' list. But by the time we realized you were there, you'd already gone. Why did you rush off like that? Why didn't you stay to see Jimmy?'

'Exactly what I said,' Knud muttered, earning himself a glare from Leila.

'Because the meeting was over and I was told to leave.' Leila shrugged, still ready to sulk. 'So I did.'

'Oh, Leila.' Sally shook her head. 'You must have known that didn't apply to you. Poor Jimmy was beside himself when he realized he'd missed you. He caught a cab and chased after you all the way to the airport.'

'Did he? But I didn't see him there?'

'No. Because he fell over somebody's luggage, hurt his head again and lost his eyesight.'

'Oh, no.' Leila was starting to understand the reason for Sally's visit. 'But he is all right?'

'Well, no. I'm afraid he isn't.'

'I hope you made him go to the hospital this time. It happened once or twice here and he wouldn't go.'

'He had no choice. We took him back to the specialist who saw him six years ago. He referred Jimmy to a neurosurgeon who removed the cause of the trouble — a brain tumour — just a few days ago.'

'A brain tumour?' Leila felt the colour draining from her face, only now beginning to imagine what her husband had been through. 'But he'll be OK?'

Sally shrugged. 'I wish I could say so for

sure. Fortunately, the tumour was benign. But although it's gone now and the pressure removed, it's still too soon to know if his eyesight can be fully restored.'

'And how is he?' Leila whispered. 'In himself?'

Sally considered the question for a moment, deciding there was no point in telling less than the truth. 'Listless. Depressed. He says what on earth is the use of a horseman who can't see? He's going to be furious with me for coming here and telling you all of this but his doctors thought you should know.'

'And they were right,' Leila said at last with a glance at her watch. 'I'm coming to Sydney with you. Now. Tonight. Pa flies to Amsterdam tomorrow so — '

'Oh no, I'm not,' said Knud. 'Not if there's trouble at home.'

'Don't be silly, Pa. You'll forfeit your ticket if you cancel at this late stage. Jimmy's already getting the best of care and there's nothing you can do.'

'But it seems so callous to go on holiday when — '

'Not at all,' Sally put in. 'Jimmy wouldn't want you to postpone your trip. We can drop you off at one of the airport hotels on our way.'

While this exchange was taking place, Leila

stabbed some numbers into her cell phone, ringing Patsy at the bistro. Succinctly, she explained what had happened and what she needed to do.

'Of course you must go,' Patsy told her. 'Jimmy needs you.'

'But I feel badly about letting you down.'

'Well, don't. I can manage and Tony should be home in a week or so. I'll get that idiot Tanya Hopkins to help out if I have to. You've been a marvellous friend, Leila, and I don't know what I'd have done without you. But now you have to look after your own.'

'Thanks, Patsy. I'll let you know how it goes.'

'Give my love to that husband of yours. He's going to cut rather a romantic figure with dark glasses and a cane.'

'Patsy!'

'Sorry — sorry. Never did know how to curb my inappropriate sense of humour. Wish Knud *bon voyage* and tell him I shall expect a postcard from Copenhagen!'

'Patsy, goodbye! I'll talk to you later.'

13

Situated high on a cliff with a magnificent view of one of Sydney's beautiful bays, Wilson Stewart's private hospital was originally an old mansion, remodelled internally for its present day use. All the same, Leila didn't like hospitals and it gave her a sinking feeling to walk up the steps to the open front doors. Sally, beside her, seemed to have no such misgivings. After all, she was bringing her brother what he most wanted and longed for — his wife.

They had said goodbye to Knud, leaving him to spend the night in a luxury hotel near the airport prior to his early morning departure. He seemed distracted, torn between anticipation of the long-awaited holiday and concern for Leila and what she might find in Sydney. Once again he said he didn't like leaving her when he felt that she needed him.

'Mr Christensen, Knud.' Sally embraced him warmly as they prepared to leave. 'You're not to worry about Leila — she'll be staying with us.'

'Oh no,' Leila put in quickly. 'I don't want to be a — '

'You're staying with us and I won't hear one word about anything else.' Sally placed an arm around her shoulders, once more addressing herself to Knud. 'Rob and I will look after her, no matter how it pans out. In the past the Kirkwoods haven't been a close family. Much as I loved my father, he could be a bully when he didn't get his own way and he caused a lot of tension in our family. I mean to change all that.'

'Thank you, Sally.' Knud returned her embrace.

'Oh, Pa.' Leila felt tears threaten now that the moment of parting had come. She hugged him tightly, suddenly afraid of losing him. 'You won't change your mind and stay there for ever? You will come back?'

'Of course,' he said. 'I've been gone from Europe too long, I can never be more than a visitor now. In any case, my home is always near you.'

'Wherever that turns out to be,' she whispered, not wanting Sally to hear.

'Now then.' He gave her a quick kiss on the forehead. 'Think only positive thoughts. I'll send you some photos as soon as I'm there.'

She smiled bravely and turned to leave, not wanting to break down and beg him, after all, not to go.

It was only later when they were alone,

awaiting their flight to Sydney, that Sally really began to talk about Jimmy.

'I couldn't have managed without him during these past few months,' she said. 'My husband might be a great accountant but he's no entrepreneur. Jimmy surprised me. There's a lot more of our dad in him than I ever thought.'

'Really?' Leila felt suddenly that the outlook was bleak. 'Then I suppose you'll want him to stay in Sydney to be a director of the company?'

'Not at all. You don't understand.' Sally was quick to reassure her. 'We needed him there during this transition stage but now we're free of the casino deal, the hotels are almost running themselves — we have very good staff. That leaves only the management of Kirkwood's Lodge and Jimmy's already put up his hand for that and wants to spend most of his time up there. He'll need to come to Sydney for the occasional board meeting but we've already decided that Rob and I will manage the hotels and Jimmy will look after the lodge.'

'Provided he's fit to do so,' Leila whispered, thinking of Patsy's thoughtless comment.

'Well, yes. But if you're going to be there with him . . . '

'Let's not get ahead of ourselves, Sally. We can't know what will happen until I've seen him.'

And now they were here, walking up carpeted stairs to the private rooms above. As they gained the second floor and walked past the nurses' station, one of them came out to speak to Sally.

'Mrs Fitzpatrick,' she said urgently. 'I'm afraid we've had rather a bad morning. Dr Stewart would like to speak to you before you go in to visit your brother.'

'Oh, God.' Sally slumped, leaning against the wall for support. 'He's not sick again, is he? He hasn't had a relapse?'

'No, no it was nothing like that. Dr Stewart asked most particularly to see you — to explain why we've transferred him to another room.'

'But Jimmy loved that room,' Sally protested. 'It was sunny and had a balcony where he could take the sea air.'

'Quite so. But Dr Stewart will explain.' Seeming anxious to be rid of them, the staff nurse knocked on the door of his office. 'I'm afraid he'll want to see only close family.' She shot a nervous glance at Leila. 'Your friend will have to wait downstairs in the visitors' lounge. There are plenty of magazines and there's also a TV.'

'This happens to be my brother's wife,' Sally told her. 'Surely she has more right than anyone to hear what Dr Stewart has to say.'

'Yes. Yes, of course.' The nurse blushed and made herself scarce when Dr Stewart summoned them into his office. He tried to smile reassuringly but his demeanour was grave. Quickly, Sally introduced Leila and started to question him without waiting for his explanation.

'What's happened? The nurse said James had a bad morning and you've had to move him. Why?'

The neurologist paused for a moment to collect his thoughts. 'Of course, you must realize he wasn't himself,' he said at last. 'In his right mind, he would never have tried to do such a thing.'

'Do what, Dr Stewart?' Leila broke in, suddenly aware that something was very wrong.

'This morning James tried to throw himself from the balcony outside his room.'

'But how could he?' Sally cried. 'He's scarcely well enough to get out of bed?'

'And that's why he didn't succeed,' Dr Stewart continued. 'He wasn't strong enough to climb over the rail. Luckily, he was seen from below by a nurse who summoned a porter to help her get him back into bed. We sedated him and moved him to a smaller room.'

'I need to see him. Now.' Leila stood up. 'This is terrible and it's all my fault.'

'No, my dear girl, it isn't.' Stewart turned his attention from Jimmy's sister. 'It's the very common reaction of an active young man who imagines his world is coming to an end because he can't see. Until now Mr Browne has been pleased with his physical progress. He has done so well that we still hope his present condition is only temporary. Most of his problems are mainly emotional now. We just have to be patient, that's all.'

'Fine!' Leila blazed at him. 'That's easy for you to say.'

'Which doesn't make it any less true.' Stewart remained unruffled. 'You can see your husband, yes. But please take it easy. Right now he needs quiet and rest. So no bouncing off the walls like a firebrand.'

'I don't . . . ' Leila began again until Sally gave her a sharp elbow in the ribs.

'Ask at the nurses' station.' The surgeon was dismissing them, his mind already on other things. 'They'll show you where he is.'

Sally offered to go with her but Leila insisted she'd rather see Jimmy alone. The room he now occupied was at the back of the house, small and dark with high windows and no tempting balcony outside a pair of French doors. She had half expected to find him tied to his bed.

He was lying on his side, apparently asleep, but Leila knew him well enough to be sure that he wasn't. His lunch remained as the orderly had left it, untouched on the tray. Leila had never seen him so pale and drawn; he looked almost as white as the bandage around his head. Underneath it, she knew his head would be shaved and stitched. *How big a hole did they have to make? And how many stitches had it taken to mend it?* Looking at him, she realized how precious he was to her and couldn't suppress a sob. He moved, turning towards the sound.

'Sally? Sal, is that you.'

'No, Jimmy, it's me,' Leila said, trying to take his hand until he stiffened and snatched it away.

'Go away, Leila.' His voice was harsh with emotion. 'I don't want you here. I told Sally I didn't want you to see me like this.'

'But I'm your wife, Jimmy. I should be here with you at this time.'

'Whatever for? I'm no use to you or to anyone and the last thing I want is your pity.' He turned as far away from her as he could without falling out of the narrow hospital bed.

'Well, great,' Leila said, close to tears now. 'I've come all this way to see you and now you won't even talk to me.'

'There's nothing to talk about. Go back to Melbourne and get your divorce. I won't fight it.'

'I don't want a divorce. I want to see the home that you love so much. I want to come and live in the Tweed Valley with you and Starshine Blue.'

'Why now?' He turned towards the sound of her voice, clearly frustrated that he couldn't see her well enough to read her expression. 'When you didn't want to before? You don't have to answer — I know. You feel sorry for me — because all my father's wealth can't give me my sight.'

'It's early days yet, Dr Stewart says — we still don't know what will happen.'

'No? I'm not deaf as well as blind, you know. They thought I was sleeping but I heard them whispering over my head. They say there's only a fifty-fifty chance that the operation will be a success.'

'So what? It isn't the end of the world. Other senses compensate.'

'Do they really?' His voice was low with bitterness. 'Would you like to try it? I don't want to survive as half a man — a part of what I was. How can I ride when I can't see where I'm going? I won't even be able to lead a horse. And I'll never set eyes on Bluey again.'

'That doesn't matter. You already know what he looks like. And you can still run your hands over him and feel him respond to your touch. Jimmy, you can't give up. Not while you still have a fighting chance.'

'But I'm tired of fighting, Leila.' Once more he turned away, pulling the bedclothes around him to hide from her. 'Leave me alone. Just go back to Melbourne and get your divorce.'

'How many times must I tell you — I don't want one! I don't even know why I went to that beastly lawyer. All my friends have been saying what a fool I was to let you go.'

'I can imagine. I can hear Patsy now telling you off for turning your back on all that lovely lolly.'

'She did, too.' Leila saw no point in denying it; she would say anything just to keep him talking, to prevent him from shutting her out. 'But she sent you her love and said you'd cut a romantic figure with dark glasses and a cane.'

For a moment she wished she hadn't been so truthful, thinking at first he was crying until she realized his shaking shoulders were due to laughter rather than tears.

'Something else, isn't she?' he said at last. 'I miss Patsy already.'

Tentatively, she took his hand and threaded her fingers through his own so that he couldn't pull away. 'We're going to fight this together, Jimmy.' She kissed his hand and then leaned forward to kiss his lips very gently and carefully, not wanting him to jerk his head away. 'Sally brought me here because she knew I'd be good for you. Nothing you can say is going to make me go away.'

'But Leila — '

'Ssh!' She kissed him with greater determination and placed her other hand on his chest to feel his heart beating under her hand. 'Those are still the same lips I love to kiss,' she whispered against them. 'And your heart still beats only for me — oh, and Starshine Blue.' She sensed that he was calmer now, no longer in the mood to push her away. 'How is the old fellow, by the way?'

'I do believe he remembered his old home. He's settled back there as if he had never left. He's already covered one of our mares. Terry seems to like it there, too, although sometimes I think he misses the excitement of race day. Clive Bannerman's foreman was pretty impressed — I shouldn't be surprised if he tries to poach him.'

Leila breathed a gentle sigh of relief. She had him looking towards the future, talking of everyday things. Now his healing could really begin.

* * *

As soon as Leila returned to his life, Jimmy's general health and well-being improved although his eyesight was still impaired. His world wasn't completely without light or movement; he could distinguish some difference between light and dark and was aware of people as shapes but that's as far as it went. Straining to see more only gave him a headache. It saddened Leila to think that those lovely brown eyes might soon become cloudy and dull, never again to look at her with humour and love.

Before he left hospital to come home to Kirkwood's Lodge, Leila went there with Sally to see what improvements could be made to accommodate his disability, making sure there were no small pieces of free-standing furniture likely to trip him. She also emailed Tina, asking her to send on the kingsize bed; it was still in the sitting-room at the cottage. Happy now to be moving on, this was the only thing she wanted from Ocean's View.

On the way there, Sally gave her a quick sketch of the household arrangements at Kirkwood's Lodge.

'Fortunately, Dad's old tartar of a housekeeper left us to get married shortly after he died. Can't tell you what a relief that was to all of us.' Sally grinned. 'Nobody liked her but at the same time no one would have found courage enough to fire her — least of all me. Right now we make do with a couple of local girls who come in twice a week to do the laundry and clean up. You can make your own arrangements. Hire a cook or someone to live in, if you want.'

'No, no.' Leila waved the suggestion away. 'I'd rather do my own cooking — I don't like the idea of servants taking over my life. My pa tried employing a housekeeper once but it didn't work out.'

'Why not?'

'The usual reason. Pa thought she was setting her cap at him, trying to seduce him with her cooking.'

'And was she?'

Leila laughed. 'We didn't keep her long enough to find out.'

On her arrival at Kirkwood's Lodge, she was given a warm welcome by both Terry and Starshine Blue although Terry's smile gave way to concern when he asked after Jimmy.

'When I first met him I was jealous because he seemed to have everything an' I didn't,' the boy said, almost to himself. 'But he's not going to be like this for ever, is he, Mrs Jim? He'll get better again?'

'We can only hope so, Terry,' she sighed. 'We just have to take it one day at a time.'

'Well, I hope he'll be home pretty soon.' Terry pulled a wry face. 'Or old Starshine Blue will go off his feed again.'

'I never knew they had so many horses here,' Leila said, looking down a long row of stalls. 'This place is a lot larger than I imagined.'

'Yes, well — old Mr Kirkwood liked to think big — or so the lads tell me But all these horses aren't ours. Quite a few of them are jus' visitin' mares.'

'I must make a start on getting to know them all.' Leila took a few steps towards the next stall, surprised when Terry stood in her path.

'Wouldn't worry about that right now,' he said. 'Things are — um — bit busy at this time of day.'

'At three in the afternoon?'

'This isn't a racing stables, Mrs Jim. Things is done different here.'

'Have to make an appointment, do I? Like everyone else?'

Terry chewed his lip, looking embarrassed. 'It's not that, but . . .'

'It's all right, I know. Jimmy will want to show me the stables himself,' she said, letting him off the hook. 'OK, I can wait.'

* * *

Everyone tried not to let Jimmy's homecoming become too emotional but his second reunion with Bluey brought tears to everyone's eyes.

'He feels just the same. Even smells just the same,' he said, leaning in to the horse who greeted him with his usual enthusiasm. 'I just wish I could really see him.'

'You will,' Leila whispered, wishing she felt more confident. 'In time I'm sure you will.'

When he could finally tear himself away from Bluey, Leila linked arms with him and asked him to walk her past the rest of the stalls. She had always thought the stables at Ocean's View were supremely well kept but here, in spite of the size of the place, there was clean sawdust and straw everywhere and the tack gleamed. Of course, there were many more hands, boys and girls, including a stud master and stable foreman, to keep everything up to scratch.

In the stable block housing the mares,

Jimmy counted two stalls down and then stood back, clearly waiting for her reaction to the horse standing within.

'Party Animal!' She clapped her hand to her mouth. 'But it can't be!'

'Not quite.' Jimmy put his arm around her shoulders and hugged her. 'I'm not a miracle worker — I can't bring him back to life for you. But this is his full sister although she's much younger, of course. I twisted Clive's arm and he gave her to us as a wedding present. Her name is Chorus Girl but we can change it to Party Girl, if you like.'

'Oh no,' Leila whispered. 'It's unlucky to change a horse's name.' For several seconds she was too choked with emotion to say anything more. 'And — and you brought her here to please me?' she managed to say at last. 'Without knowing if I'd ever come here to see her?'

'Not quite. I did it for me, too. I had to have faith that we'd be together again one day. Otherwise, there's no point to any of this.'

She closed her eyes, squeezing his arm. Really, she would have liked to kiss him passionately right there and then but she was all too aware of the amused and curious glances of the young men and women employed to work in this constant hive of activity. So she patted the horse instead, stroking her soft yet whiskery muzzle. The mare snickered, pushing at Leila's pockets for a treat.

'Oh dear,' she said. 'And I don't have anything for you.'

'I do.' Jimmy pulled a small, hard apple out of his pocket. 'Here you are, greedy girl.'

* * *

Appreciating that Leila and Jimmy would need some time alone to become accustomed to living together again, Sally and Rob made excuses to leave at once, returning to Sydney that same night. They had the house to themselves as most of their lads resided in the dormitory and canteen quarters attached to the stables, the girls coming in every day. From the outset Jimmy's father had decided the girls should live out, realizing it would be asking for trouble to have teenage boys and girls with raging hormones living in close proximity to each other. Nor did he want to employ a matron to police their behaviour. Everyone knew the occasional romantic attachment would slip through the net; a girl would be sneaked into a dormitory or a couple would return from a lunch break, pink and breathless after a quick encounter in the hayloft but it was easier for everyone to ignore them, pretending not to see.

Jimmy was delighted that Leila had sent for their bed and he ran his hands over the patchwork quilt that Val had been so reluctant to sell him, remembering all the textures and colours. But when the moment came to actually get into it together, they were both suddenly shy.

'Leila, what is it?' he said, sensing her tension and pausing even as he moved to draw her close. He was only just beginning to sense her moods without being able to see her expressions. 'It's me, isn't it? And no wonder — I must be a sight like Frankenstein's monster with all those scars and a baldy head?'

'No, of course not.' She ran her hand gently over his scalp where a fuzz of vigorous new hair was already growing to cover the scars. 'It won't be long before you have an entirely new head of hair.'

'And I'm not frail, if that's what's worrying you. I won't break.'

'It's not that, either. It — just feels a bit strange, that's all. Here we are in the bed that we chose together and it should be as familiar as coming home. Yet somehow it doesn't. Everything seems so different here and so new.'

'The bottom line being that you don't feel married to me any more?'

'Jimmy! What a terrible thing to say. Of course I feel married to you.'

'Yes, but there's something missing, isn't there? You need to feel married to James Kirkwood as well as to Jimmy Flynn. I've been thinking maybe we ought to renew our vows.'

'What?' She was beginning to wonder if more than a tumour had been removed from his brain. 'People don't do that until they've been married for years. Our wedding was just a few months ago.'

'Well, that's true. But when I look back on it, Leila, I feel very guilty about our wedding day — remembering that grumpy vicar and the bleak atmosphere in the church with no flowers. No sense of occasion, at all. If it hadn't been for Patsy, you wouldn't even have had a reception. I want to redress the balance and give you a glorious wedding day — even if I can't see any more than shapes or shadows. It doesn't have to be too formal — we don't need a big reception or even a church this time. We could say our vows before a marriage celebrant in the gardens here.'

'Yes and Terry can bring along Starshine Blue to be your best man,' she joked, still not entirely sure he was serious.

'Now that is a good idea. I wish I'd thought of it.'

'You're serious, aren't you? You really want to do this for me?' And as she leaned forward to kiss him, she hoped he wouldn't be aware of the tears in her eyes. He sensed or heard them in her voice and took her face in his hands, gently wiping them away with his fingers.

'From now on, Leila, I don't want to hear you cry,' he said. 'Except when you're happy.'

14

A bower covered in white lilies and roses had been erected in the large, open front garden at Kirkwood's Lodge and, although Leila and Jimmy had protested that they wanted to keep the occasion small and intimate, Sally had taken charge of all the arrangements, hired a marquee, employed caterers and invited all the people she thought should have been at her brother's wedding the first time. Patsy and Tony, not wanting to miss the event, had taken the rare step of closing the bistro and come to spend a week on the Gold Coast nearby.

The most notable guest was Clive Bannerman, still complaining bitterly of his own daughter's marriage. 'You should see that bloke,' he grumbled to Jimmy. 'He can give me five years at least and has no voice — can't even hold a proper tune. What was she thinking? And to think she let you slip through her fingers, as well.' He sighed, shaking his leonine head. 'If only I'd known who you were, things might've been very different.' Suddenly, he realized Leila was listening to what he was saying, staring at him with raised eyebrows. 'Yeah well, sorry Leila. But you know what I mean. Dianne's loss is your gain.'

Jimmy squeezed her hand, warning her not to take offence at the old man's words. Whatever opinion anyone had of Dianne, Clive still thought the sun shone out of her eyes.

The marriage celebrant arrived well before time, a youthful forty-something lady with a porcelain complexion and whose abundant, shoulder-length hair was completely white. She was dressed from head to toe in white linen, too, making Leila pleased she had opted for loose-fitting floating georgette in a vibrant wisteria blue.

'The marriage celebrant. What does she look like?' Jimmy whispered, unable to make out more than a dim white shape standing in front of them.

'An angel, actually,' Leila whispered back. 'And with curly white hair. All she needs is a pair of big, white wings to make the picture complete.'

He laughed softly, making her smile.

The marriage celebrant clapped her hands, calling for silence and motioning everyone to draw near to hear James and Leila make their renewed promises. She knew the story of James' alter ego as Jimmy Flynn and sympathized with their need to reaffirm their vows and set the record straight.

'Friends and relatives of Leila and James,' she called in a strong voice, smiling at them. 'You are summoned on this happy occasion to hear them confirm their wedding vows and once more pledge themselves to each other. James — perhaps you would like to speak first?'

Jimmy turned towards Leila who placed her hands in his to reassure him, making up for the fact that he couldn't see her.

'Leila, I love you,' he said simply. 'I think I loved you from the first moment I saw you standing in your father's kitchen with your arms folded, sizing me up, as suspicious of Starshine Blue as you were of me. And later, when we learned to know each other better and grew closer, I couldn't bear to think of a life without you. And that — that is why I was afraid to tell you the truth of my heritage, of all this.' He made a gesture, encompassing the house and grounds. 'On so many occasions you spoke to me of preferring a simple life. But if you're brave enough to take me on again and give me a second chance, I promise to devote the rest of my life to you. Please make me the happiest man in the world by saying you will.'

'Ohh!' Leila said as her eyes once more

blurred with tears.

'Leila?' Smiling, the marriage celebrant turned towards her.

'That was so beautiful,' she said. 'It has driven all that I was going to say right out of my head.' There was a concerted groan from the crowd. 'But if I were to get started on all the many reasons why I love James here, we shouldn't get to the wedding feast before midnight. I do love you, Jimmy Flynn and I'm learning to love James Kirkwood, too. How many woman get two devoted husbands for the price of one?' There was a soft murmur of laughter from the listening crowd. 'But to be perfectly serious for a moment — yes, Jimmy, I will accept you to be my husband again and promise that I will do all that I can to make you happy.'

'Then,' said the marriage celebrant, 'it's time to exchange your new rings.'

Having expected to receive the same plain wedding ring she had worn before, Leila gasped with surprise when she saw the beautiful eternity ring that came with it, with diamonds and sapphires, catching the light in the sun.

'Now why didn't I think of buying you another ring?' she whispered.

'Doesn't matter,' he said. 'I'm just as happy to wear the old one again.'

'And now . . . ' The celebrant brought the simple ceremony to a close. 'In my capacity as a licensed celebrant in the State of New South Wales, I now pronounce you husband and wife. James, you may kiss your bride.'

Jimmy leaned towards Leila but suddenly he shivered, let go of her hands and removed his dark glasses, only to wince and replace them again.

'Jimmy, what's wrong?' Leila felt a sense of rising panic. 'Has something happened? Are you in pain?'

'Only because I shouldn't have taken off the sunglasses — the light was too bright. Leila, I think I can see! It's as if a curtain of fog is lifting and my eyesight is coming back.'

'Are you sure?' Leila felt stunned, not quite able to believe such a miracle had occurred and half afraid that the curtain would fall again, plunging him into further despair.

'Yes. Yes, I can see you — and you look so beautiful today. What did I ever do to deserve you? And yes . . . ' He turned towards the marriage celebrant. 'I can see the angel, too.'

'Angel?' The woman laughed, slightly embarrassed by his words.

'Indeed, you must be. To perform such a miracle as this.'

This seemed to be the signal for everyone to crowd around them, offering kisses and congratulations. Sally nodded towards the waiting staff to start serving champagne.

'Forgive me,' Jimmy whispered to his bride. 'I'll be back in just a moment but there's someone I have to see.'

'Oh Jimmy, you're not thinking of going to the stables — in a tuxedo?' She gave him a wry smile, shaking her head. But of course he was already gone.

Five minutes later, he was back, leading Starshine Blue who raised his head majestically, playing to his admiring audience as usual. The crowd acknowledged his arrival with cheers and applause and if the handsome animal was surprised at not being called upon to race, he certainly didn't show it. Jimmy kept him by his side for the whole afternoon and Leila had to put up with many quips that Starshine Blue might be sharing their marriage bed that night. He stayed until the last of the guests were leaving and Terry came to take him away.

'Can I have a word?' he said to Jimmy and Leila. 'I wouldn't bother you if it wasn't important. But maybe I shouldn't talk business on your wedding day?'

'Spill it, Terry.' Jimmy smiled. 'If you don't, we'll only spend our wedding night wondering what it is.'

'It's Mr Bannerman. He's offered me . . . '

Terry began, only to break off. 'Look, if you really want me to stay here with Bluey, I will. You gave me the best job I've ever had in my life an' I jus' love the old boy but — '

'But you're wasted here as a stable hand. You like riding track work and miss the excitement of taking horses to the track.' Jimmy completed the sentence for him.

'Well, yeah.' Terry looked relieved, his next words coming out in a rush. 'An' Mr Bannerman says he's jus' lost a rider an' then Mr Kelso told him about me. He says there's a job waitin' for me down at his place if I — '

'Terry, go and with our blessing.' Leila kissed the lad, making him blush. 'We both understand you're not really happy away from the track.'

'Thanks!' Terry's face lit up. 'I'll go an' catch up with Mr Bannerman an' tell him before he leaves.'

When everyone else had gone, including the caterers and finally Sally and Rob, Leila and Jimmy sat in comfortable chairs, looking out across the many paddocks of Kirkwood's Lodge. The last of the champagne had been drunk and they were enjoying long glasses of iced water now. The sun was setting over the cane fields and the distant mountains, the nightly chorus of frogs and insects almost deafening. They couldn't have sat there at this time of the evening without a mosquito zapper.

'I've always loved sitting here watching the sun go down.' Jimmy sighed his contentment. 'I never really expected to see it again.'

'It's beautiful. A fitting end to a perfect day.'

'You *are* going to be happy here, Leila, aren't you?' He felt he had to ask, to be quite sure. 'You won't miss the island?'

'I can always go and stay with Patsy for a while, if I do.' Leila grinned mischievously. 'She's already promised to be a frequent visitor here at Kirkwood's Lodge.'

'Long as Tony comes too, to keep her in order.' Jimmy pulled a wry face. 'Fond as I am of Patsy, I like her in small doses.'

'Are you hungry?' Leila sprang to her feet. 'All of a sudden, I'm starving. I could murder an egg on toast. What about you?'

'Not me. After all we put away at the wedding feast, I couldn't eat another thing.' He looked at her anxiously, glancing at her burgeoning bosom and the curve of her stomach under the diaphanous dress, unsure whether to voice his thoughts or not. 'Leila, I don't want you to take this the wrong way, but you're not putting on weight, are you?'

She laughed richly, making him notice that along with the new radiance of her complexion, she had the very slightest of double chins. 'I am, indeed. I must have put on at least a couple of kilos since you left me in Melbourne. Don't you like it?'

'It's OK, I suppose.' He didn't know what to say without offending her. 'But I wouldn't like to think you'd put on a whole lot more.'

'Oh, I'm sure I will,' she said nonchalantly. 'It's in the genes, you see. We Christensens are already tall and we get quite enormous when we're carrying a baby.'

'A what?' He froze. 'Did you say what I think you did?'

'Uh-huh. I just told you — we're having a baby. Two, actually. Twins are quite common in our family.'

Jimmy continued to stare at the sunset, for a moment too full of emotion to speak. In the space of a day, both his eyesight and his wife had been restored to him and now he was about to be a father too.

'Well, say something,' she said at last, unable to bear the ongoing silence.

'When?'

'September, of course. Don't you know most babies are conceived around Christmas time?'

'September! And soon after that we'll be seeing the birth of Bluey's first foal.'

'Well, if that's all it means to you!'

Emotionally fragile, tears sprang to Leila's eyes and she turned away, meaning to go to the kitchen and have a good cry. Raging hormonal changes had much to answer for. Before she could get there, Jimmy caught up with her in two quick strides, taking her rigid form into his arms. Although she murmured objections, he started to kiss her and wouldn't stop until she relaxed in his arms.

'You can't need any more proof that I love you,' He whispered against her ear. 'Not after today. And you don't have to be jealous of Bluey. However much I do love him, I will always love you and our children more.'

'And you don't think it's too soon for us to start a family?'

'Bit late to worry about that now. Of course it isn't too soon — this is the best wedding present I could have wished for.'

Suddenly, her smile was radiant again. 'Come on,' she said. 'Let's see what we can find in the kitchen. I'm eating for three now and I'm starved.'

Other titles published by The House of Ulverscroft:

RED FOR DANGER

Heather Graves

Leaving behind a career in an American soap opera, Foxie Marlowe returns to Melbourne to comfort her recently widowed mother and take over her father's racing stables. However, she learns that during her father's illness, Daniel Morgan — the son of a family friend and the man with whom she once had an affair — rescued the business. Foxie believes that Daniel has taken advantage and stolen her inheritance, until he convinces her to join him as a business partner. Ignoring her lawyer's advice, she invests both her money and emotions in Daniel. But can she really trust him?

FLYING COLOURS

Heather Graves

With a broken romance behind her and a promising future ahead Corey O'Brien intends to concentrate on her chosen career. She certainly doesn't expect to come to the attention of someone like Mario Antonello, a racehorse owner and heir to a fashion house . . . Their first meeting isn't friendly so she is surprised by the interest he shows in her later. It all seems too much and it will take a while for Corey to find out the truth. Then she discovers a shocking secret and feels she must turn her back on him forever.

GLISTER

John Burnside

Leonard and his friends, living in the decaying and industrial ruin that is the coastal community of Innertown, exist in a state of suspended terror. Every year or so, a boy from their school disappears, vanishing into the wasteland of the old chemical plant. Nobody knows where these boys go, or whether they are alive or dead, and without evidence the authorities claim they are simply runaways. The town policeman, Morrison, knows otherwise. He was involved in the cover-up of one boy's murder, and he believes all the boys have been killed. And although seriously compromised, Morrison — along with the local children — wants to find the killer's identity.

MERCY

Lara Santoro

When Italian-American journalist Anna arrives in Nairobi she knows that the daily atrocities she reports on will be upsetting, but she has to battle her own personal demons too. To escape the violence that surrounds her, Anna drinks too much and gets ever more entangled with two men: Michael, a fellow war-correspondent, and Nick, a wealthy coffee farmer — each of them hard to resist, each of them hard to love. And then Mercy enters her life — ostensibly as her maid, but immediately becoming Anna's most adamant judge, her harshest critic, and gradually — painfully, also her counsellor and her friend.

DRESDEN, TENNESSEE

Carolyn Slaughter

New York, February 13, 2006. Kurt Altman, a young man living in New York, suffers a sudden and inexplicable attack of amnesia. Convinced of an imminent bombing attack he flees the city, and heads south, drawn there for reasons he doesn't understand. On a plane he meets business psychologist Hannah Brown, the daughter of an immigrant Jewish family. A powerful sexual attraction, and their links with a German past, draws them together. Soon Hannah is drawn into Kurt's search for his identity, which ends in Dresden, Tennessee. And there he encounters a stranger who holds the key to unlocking his memory . . .

FLIGHT

Sherman Alexie

The journey for *Flight's* young hero begins as he's about to commit a massive act of violence. At the moment of the decision, he finds himself shot back through time to resurface in the body of an FBI agent during the civil rights era, where he sees why 'Hell is Red River, Idaho, in the 1970s'. Red River is only the first stop in an eye-opening trip through moments in American history. He will continue travelling back to inhabit the body of an Indian child during the battle at Little Bighorn and then ride with an Indian tracker in the nineteenth century before materialising as an airline pilot jetting through the skies today. During these travels through time, his refrain grows: 'Who's to judge?'